History began some three thousand years ago. All that has happened lies within that time, from the first day of the world, till now. The myths of creation vary little from one land to another. My people say the creatures of the earth first appeared in Albion, where they sinned against the Creator, and were cast out upon the world. The Vikonen tell the story in a different manner, as do the Nicieans. Each, however, include the Dark Isle of Albion in their tale. They are right to do so, but not for the reasons they imagine. I have been to Albion, and I know its terrible secret. There, indeed, is where we began—but the rest of the story is a lie. The sin is Man's, not ours, for it was he who fashioned us from beasts to mirror his own sad history.

Why did he do this thing? That, I cannot say. Perhaps he gained some pleasure watching the shame and glory of his race relived again. . . .

Aldair, Across the Misty Sea

Neal Barrett, Jr.

DAW Books, Inc.
Donald A. Wollheim, Publisher
1633 Broadway
New York, N.Y. 10019

FOR RUTH,

who has a Rhalgorn of her own
around the house, and has shown
great patience in the matter ...

FIRST PRINTING, MARCH 1980

1 2 3 4 5 6 7 8 9

 DAW TRADEMARK REGISTERED
U.S. PAT. OFF. MARCA
REGISTRADA. HECHO EN U.S.A.

PRINTED IN U.S.A.

Prologue

———◆—————◆—————◆———

"More than once since I began a'venturing, I have envied the lot of lesser creatures. I know for certain now the better one perceives the world around him, the more pain and misery he is likely to encounter. We could all learn a lesson from the turnip, who handles his affairs quite sensibly. He is warmed by the sun and cooled by the summer rain. His feet are comfortably rooted in one place, and he has no desire to sniff out trouble in another garden. The common mouse is similarly blessed, and has the sense to know it. I have yet to hear of one who left a sack of corn behind to search for hungry vipers.

"Yet, those of us with finer heads on our shoulders eagerly leave the warmth of our homes to seek death, privation, and other ills wherever we can find them. This is sometimes called the search for truth and knowledge—but mostly by those who have seldom ventured more than a league from their own front doors. Those of us who have traveled a good deal further have another, less charitable name for it.

"I can honestly say that I have done more than my share of wandering. In a few short years, I have been slave, scholar and master of ships. I have played no small part in the death of two great empires. I have nearly been eaten whole by the shapeless thing that guards the Great River. I have even soared above the earth like a large ungainly bird. The less said about that, the better.

"Finally, I have come to know the handiwork of Man, in the sad and fearful land of Merrkia, across the Misty Sea. The terrible secret of that race has come to light at last, though

5

it is a thing I can scarcely fathom even now. And if I have learned nothing more in my travels, I can say in all truth that I am proud to be the beast I am. . . ."

—Aldair, late of the Venicii,
adrift on the Darker Sea

One

We have a saying in the Eubirones: One Vikonen is a crowd, two are a small village. The saying goes no further, for few would care to imagine more than a pair of these great creatures at a time. In my own land, we know the Vikonen well, for their longboats come to trade in the northern ports of Gaullia every spring, as soon as the frozen sea will let them through. They drive a hard bargain over a load of goods, and take pleasure in cheating other races out of a single copper coin. It is not overly wise to catch them at this, for it is a large Gaullian indeed who reaches the belly of a small Vikonen warrior.

I have come to have a special liking for these creatures, for the best of them is the captain of my vessel and perhaps the finest seaman in the world. More than that, Signar-Haldring is a blood-companion, a true and loyal friend. Through him, I have learned much about his people, and in all honesty there is a great deal more to these furry giants than meets the eye. People in the southern provinces have little understanding of the Vikonen warrior, for they have only seen him swarming aboard their vessels with a bloody war-axe in hand. Not the best moment, perhaps, for a fair appraisal.

In spite of their awesome strength and warlike nature, I have found the Vikonen to be a friendly, even-tempered folk. And while they will brood over nothing at times, they come quickly to life at the smell of barley beer, or a fight in the making. To the best of my knowledge, they find both activities equally appealing.

Thus, I thought I truly understood the ways of the Vikonen. But that was before I met the people of Raadnir. These creatures are a breed apart from those who ply the seas from the cold port of Vhiborg. Even Signar found them strange—and they, in turn, did little to make him feel at home. He was bewildered, and more than a little angry, for the Vikonen take great pride in who they are and where they come from.

"I'll tell you this," he said darkly, wrapping his big fist around a mug of ale, "it's no proper way to treat your own kind, and that's for certain. Why, if I didn't know better, Aldair, I'd say they wasn't true Vikonen at all, but somethin' that just—*looks* like 'em." He shook his broad head and made a face. "Creator's Eyes, they don't even *smell* right!"

"I'd not hold that against them," mused Rhalgorn. "Smelling right has ever been a failing among the Vikonen."

Signar bristled. "If I was you, rabbit-breath, I'd think more'n once 'fore I talked about other folks, and their manner of smelling."

Rhalgorn laughed, that peculiar coughing sound that passes for laughter among the Stygianns. Signar-Haldring growled deep in his chest, then turned away to stare balefully at the shores of Raadnir.

There was little enough to see there. A rocky plain came down to meet the sea, sloping gently from the barren lands above. The earth was littered with small round stones, as far as the eye could follow. None were much larger than pebbles, for the bigger specimens had been collected over the years to build the low stone huts that sheltered the people of Raadnir from the cold. At best, it was a bitter, colorless place to live. One did not have to wonder why such folk had forgotten their beginnings—there was little here to keep the past alive. Signar saw this clearly, but he could not bring himself to believe that the warrior-seamen of Vikonea could come to stink of herring, and burn the dung of snowdeer in their fires. We had discussed this more than once, but once is seldom enough for a Vikonen.

"The people of Raadnir are what they are, and doubtless what they will ever be," I said again. "If they have forgotten the call of the sea and the feel of a fine blade, there's reason enough for it. Nevertheless, their fathers sprang from the fjords of Vhiborg Deep, as did yours. This is as true as rain, whether you like it or not."

"Their *fathers'* fathers, and then some," Signar muttered. "They're a long time gone from where they started."

"That may be so. Still—"

"Aldair—" He turned his head to face me, short ears flat

against the wind. "I *know* what you're about, old friend, and I'll tell you once again you're wrong as you can be. If you're waitin' for Sergrid Bad-Beard to point the way west, why, we'll be squattin' here till the sea freezes tight about our hull." He sniffed the air and let a chill breeze ruffle his heavy pelt. "Which, by the way, isn't all that many weeks away, if I know the smell of weather."

He was right, of course. Winter was on its way to the gray land of Raadnir. And I did not intend to be on hand when it arrived. I would plough the Misty Sea without direction if I had to, though it was not a choice I greatly welcomed.

"Give it another chance," I asked him. "Share a mug or two with the fellow and spin him a yarn of pillage and plunder."

"Ha!" Signar twitched his nose in disgust. "The ale's not a proper drink at all, and smells a lot more like fish droppin's than good northern malt. And tales of old Vhiborg ain't about to soften up Sergrid Bad-Beard, Aldair. Why, he sits there dumb as a toad on a stump, like he don't believe a word I'm saying!"

I caught Rhalgorn's eye and tried desperately to hold a sober face—both of us burst out laughing at once. Signar gave us a sour look. "No one's supposed to *believe* Vikonen yarns," I told him. "Least of all another Vikonen. The marvel of 'em is in the telling!"

"Or sitting all the way through one without leaping into the sea," added Rhalgorn. "Even a Lord of the Lauvectii lacks the courage for that."

I tried very hard to fill the Vikonen's mug again, but missed the thing completely and soaked the deck with ale. Rhalgorn, rolling his eyes about like a mad hare, did not help matters at all. Signar-Haldring was not certain whether he was in on the joke, or part of it. Finally, he granted us a sullen grin and raised his great bulk to the deck.

"I'll give it another try, then," he said darkly, "for it looks as if the fate of the whole expedition rests on good Signar, for certain. In the end, damned if it ain't them that has the most to do gets the more thrown at 'em."

"We know you'll do your best," I assured him. Signar growled deep in his chest and stomped away.

"If worse comes to worse," Rhalgorn called after him, "try your charms on that fair maiden you've been eyeing. The one near as big as a haybarn."

Signar stopped dead in his tracks, hackles rising on his broad shoulders. For a long moment, he simply stood there, pondering the joy of tossing Rhalgorn into the cold waters. Then, he made his way forward, shaking the deck beneath his boots. Before long, we could hear him bellowing for a crewman to get a boat over the side.

"That was not a particularly wise choice of words," I told Rhalgorn.

"No? It seemed most appropriate at the time."

"It would, to you. Stygianns seldom know when to leave well enough alone. It is not in their character to do so. Which is why they are always in one sort of trouble or another."

Rhalgorn grinned, showing his long teeth. "Only a warrior of the Venicii could know how much trouble a Stygiann can be. We have kept your snouts west of the River Rheinus for longer than you'd care to remember."

"If it comes to that," I said, "there are enough gray pelts warming the floors of the Eubirones to show why your people greatly prefer the *east* side of the river. There's no—"

Rhalgorn held up a hand and grinned. "You've seen her, haven't you?"

"What? Seen who?"

"Why, the fair Bruhngella, who else? Fat-fur's love among the good folk of Raadnir. Aldair, she'd truly make a fine mate for a fair-sized oak."

I glanced nervously over my shoulder, uncertain Signar was truly on his way across the waters. "Some day," I warned the Stygiann, "good fat-fur is going to forget you're only the *second* Lord of the Lauvectii he hasn't shortened with an axe on sight. As for this Bruhn-whatever, I would not expect the Vikonen female to resemble either a radish or a hare, Rhalgorn. Females generally look a great deal like the males of their race, which makes good sense to me."

Rhalgorn made a face. "Please, Aldair—do not mention hares in my presence. Sometimes, I can near taste one, ripe from a good week's hanging in the crook of my favorite tree."

"Ripe is one word for it," I said. "If you're hungry, which I'd guess you are since supper's been over near half an hour, there's still a roast of snowdeer down below."

The Stygiann's eyes sparkled with interest. "That's the most worthy idea I've heard all day. A snowdeer is not a hare, by any means, but it will suffice till one comes along. Though only the gods know when *that* might be." He stood, casting a disparaging eye at the dull horizon, then at me. "Aldair, wherever it is we are going, I trust we will go there soon. This is not a seemly place to be."

With that, he shook the wind from his fur and made his way below.

Two

To Rhalgorn, anything that is not found in the dark forests of the Lauvectii is by nature unseemly, for a Stygiann is not the most tolerant of creatures. For once, though, I found it hard to fault him. I, too, could think of a number of places I would rather be than the bleak shores of Raadnir. They say the farther one roams from his homeland, the sweeter it seems to be. This may be so, for in my mind's eye the broad meadows of the Eubirones are shaded a near impossible green.

Such memories are a comfort to the traveler, and it is all too easy to forget that much of what we left behind may be just that—fond memories, and nothing more. The terrible red eye of the Man-thing has turned the heart of Rhemia to a wasteland, and if its deadly aura of fear has not yet touched the north, I am certain its effects have been felt there in other ways. The Rhemian Lords cared little for their subjects in the best of times—I cannot imagine chaos and disaster have made them kinder masters.

Thus, I do not think we will see again such days as we remember. The thing that lies in Rhemia's streets has closed one door forever, and opened wide another. Surely, the ghost of Man laughs from his grave at the folly of his creatures. We have learned what we were, and what we have become—but we have paid a heavy price in the knowing.

That is the thing about gray and dismal landscapes—they foster thoughts to match their somber color. I have found that a good tart wine will sometimes counter this mood, and as I knew where such a remedy could be found, I hastily headed for it.

It would be hard to find two more different creatures than Thareesh and the fair Corysia. Niceans are blood-enemies of all things Rhemian, and Corysia, of course, is the niece of

Titus Augustus himself. However, as none of us aboard the *Ahzir al'Rhaz* care a whit for what we are *supposed* to think or do, I found the pair together in my cabin, soaking up the warmth of the big iron stove. Both of them come from the warm lands around the Southern Sea, and have no love for winter weather.

Corysia looked up as I entered, a question beginning in her eyes. "There is no news of great interest," I told her. "The folk of Raadnir remain as distant as ever."

"That is news of a sort," sighed Thareesh, "though not the kind one is eager to hear. If I did not know better, Aldair, I would say the sun has never blessed this land. I cannot believe the shores of Raadnir have felt the warmth of a cold Niciean night."

I grinned at him and dropped down beside Corysia. "Thareesh, a *bright* midsummer's day here would not match the coolest cellar in all Chaarduz."

"I am afraid this is true."

"However, if it will make you feel any better, old friend, I will tell you this—I do not intend to spend another day in this place if Sergrid Bad-Beard turns us down again."

Corysia brightened. "And you said there was no news of interest. Nothing could interest me more!"

I told them we had asked Signar-Haldring to make one last effort to gain the ear of Raadnir's leader. "If he fails, we sail to the south on our own, with all three ships. There is a land there somewhere, for I saw it clearly marked in the towers of the Avakhar."

"Then we will find it," Thareesh said solemnly. "With or without the help of Sergrid Bad-Beard. For I am certain luck is with us, Aldair." His eyes held me a long moment—cold black agates in a near expressionless face. Those who have never lived among the Nicieans find them frightening to behold. At first glance, they seem to have no true features at all, merely slits and gashes where a nose and mouth and ears should be. Moreover, their slim green forms are completely hairless, covered with tiny scales instead of fur or hair. Appearances aside, however, Nicieans are much the same as other folk, with both good and bad among them.

"I am feeling much better already," said Thareesh, filling his mug with hot wine, "for I am certain we will be sailing for the south by morning—none the wiser, but a great deal closer to the sun."

"I hope you are not expecting the heat of the Great Desert anytime soon," I warned him. "If Signar's reckoning is true, we are on a latitude roughly the same as Vikonea. It will take a fair bit of sailing before you are properly warm."

Thareesh peered out from the heavy folds of his cloak. "Thank you for those reassuring words, Aldair. Suddenly, I am not as comfortable as I imagined. If you will excuse me, I will go to my cabin and search for more blankets."

"There are not enough blankets in the world to warm a Niciean," laughed Corysia.

"You are right in that," he admitted. "As Rhalgorn would say, this is not a seemly place to be." A near-smile cut the thin line of his mouth. "You see, Aldair? There are times when even a Stygiann speaks the truth—"

"—whether he intends to or not," I finished.

He nodded politely to Corysia, and left us, the thin green whip of his tail clinging tightly to his legs against the cold.

I filled my mug from atop the stove, and freshened hers. "You are not very talkative today, Corysia. If I remember correctly, highborn Rhemian ladies have a good deal to say about everything."

"That they do," she said tartly, "and if one were here, you'd know it for certain, Aldair. However, we ordinary females who follow one-eared warriors about the world fear our masters' wrath and wisely say nothing."

I laughed and tousled her hair. "As Signar fears a keg of ale, you do! As for this business of the ear, Lady, I'll thank you not to speak of it again. It's enough that good Rhalgorn offers daily to slice the one remaining, to keep my head in balance."

Corysia closed one eye and studied me thoughtfully. "I had not noticed before, Aldair, but I do believe he is right. Perhaps there is a cleaver in the galley—"

She made to get up and I pulled her to me, shutting her sudden laughter with a kiss. Her arms went about me and we held each other a long moment, saying nothing.

In truth, I would not have believed that such a time could ever be. Much has happened between us since that bright fair morning I took her from the Rhemians. Hatred and disdain have turned to love, but this did not come quickly, for Corysia

was not brought up to care for ill-kempt Venicii warriors. I
was outcast, barbarian and heretic in the bargain. My only
companions were creatures straight from a Rhemian child's
nightmare. Not the best beginning, perhaps, for an affair of
the heart.

Nevertheless, by some great miracle there is love between
us now. And though I have learned to know Corysia well, I
will not soon forget her as she was that moment in far Duroc-
tium—proud, haughty, sitting astride her mount as well as any
soldier. Truly, I had never seen a lovelier vision. Black liquid
eyes set close above a perky little snout; sharp downy ears
tipped with a touch of pink. Her fine figure was covered in
soft auburn hair, and the manner of her dress left little to the
imagination. The green satin gown fell about her shoulders and
curved to her belly in neat half-circles, barely concealing the
soft row of breasts on either side. Quite a sight indeed for a
lad raised on the plains of the Eubirones. In some respects, I
have come a long way in the past few years.

Corysia raised her head from my shoulder and touched my
cheek. "And where did you journey with your thoughts, Master Aldair? You have not been aboard the *Ahzir*, for certain."

"You had better not ask," I told her, "for we do not have
time at the moment to discuss the subject thoroughly."

Corysia looked amused. "Ah, I see."

"Indeed you do."

"Your thoughts were not too far from mine, then."

"It often seems to work that way. And a fine arrangement
it is, if you ask me."

"Except when there is not time for further—discussion."

"Yes. Except for that."

She laughed, then stood and moved to the small port that
looked out upon the bleak landscape of Raadnir. She watched
for a long moment without speaking, then turned to face me.
"Aldair—what do you think we will find there?"

"Where? In the land to the west, you mean? I cannot say,
Corysia. I only know that it is there, and that I must seek
it out."

"Must, Aldair?" I caught the question in her eyes.

"There are dreams that lie, and dreams that speak the truth.
This one does not lie. It has come to me more than once since
we left the Southern Sea. As well you know."

"I do not doubt you," she said gently.

I realized there was an edge to my words I had not intended. "I'm sorry—I know you do not. I would not blame you
if you did. Nor the others, either."

"It's a Man-place, isn't it?"

I hesitated before I spoke. "It is a Man-place. Or was."
There was more, as she knew. But I would go no further, and
she did not pursue it. I would have filled the silence between
us, but could find no words to fit.

"Aldair—I do understand. What you say, and what you do
not."

"Good," I told her, "for I am not always certain that *I* do,
Corysia."

We both looked up, for the moment was suddenly broken
by the sound of heavy boots making their way below. They
could belong to none but Signar-Haldring, unless a pair of
great oaks had come aboard. Then, his giant form burst
through the door, scattering fur and frost all about.

"I'm damned if I know what came over him," he shouted,
"but he'll do it, Aldair. He's heard of lands to the south, and
he'll point the way!"

"What?" I came quickly to my feet. "Sergrid Bad-Beard?"

Signar nodded and caught his breath, reaching gratefully
for the hot mug Corysia offered.

"He'll see us. You an' me, in about an hour. And more'n
that, there's to be a *feast* of some kind, and everybody's to
come. Figure *that* one, if you can."

I am sure I looked as bewildered as Signar and Corysia. "I
don't much care for this sudden turn-about. It is not like
Sergrid Bad-Beard."

"No," he agreed, "it ain't, for sure. An' I don't like it any
more'n you do."

"A *feast*, you say?"

"Sure enough."

Corysia said it for us all. "I guess we don't have a great
deal of choice in the matter, do we?"

Three

The presence of obstacles in one's path is a natural condition, and no great cause for alarm. The time to start worrying is when those obstacles are suddenly removed, and the way seems free and clear. Thus, I viewed Sergrid's change of heart as ominous, at best. My companions shared this concern, most especially Signar, who had come to know the people of Raadnir better than the rest of us.

"It don't look right, Aldair," he told me. Or, later: "I don't like the smell of this business. . . ." There were a good dozen other dark warnings designed to cheer me for the task ahead.

Nevertheless, there being nothing else for it, we soon found ourselves in the damp stone hut of Sergrid Bad-Beard himself. There was little to see there, for it was not the lodging of a chieftain in the world we'd left behind. There were snowdeer skins on the walls, a collection of dirty clay pots and nothing more—save the sputtering fish-oil lamp and a smell that would shame a Rhemian sewer. The one sign of Sergrid's high position was a rude wooden table, a great log laboriously split in two. Trees are rare as gold in this land, and I guessed it was the only one of its kind near about.

Our host wasted no time on amenities. There was a pot of ale on the table, and it was assumed we could see it there. "Here's what you're wanting," he grunted, pulling a dark bundle from under the table, "though why any right thinkin' creature would care to go to such a place is past my understanding."

He jerked a binding loose and let the bundle fly open, then smoothed it flat and set the lamp on one corner. "Here's Raadnir," he said, laying a big thumb to the north, "and down here's the place you're askin' about."

I followed his finger past open seas far to the south and slightly eastward. It was a rather disappointing map—wriggly lines on the back of a scraped piece of skin, the whole of it near obscured by the grime of the ages. Still, the people of Raadnir were Vikonens, and even the least of these folk are born with the smell of the sea.

"Do you know anything of this place," I asked him, "what it's called, or what's to be found there?"

He ignored me, and put his answer to Signar. Sergrid's ancestors had come to this land long ago, and their descendants had forgotten other races. All save Signar-Haldring were a wonder to him, and he was not quite sure what to make of us.

"I know of it, all right," Sergrid frowned. "More'n a body'd care to."

"And what would that be?" Signar asked him.

"That it's not a place to go huntin' for, as I said before."

"There's danger to face? Bad seas?"

"All of that, I'd guess. And likely more."

Signar gave me a quick, puzzled glance. "You'd *guess*, you say? Then you've not been there yourself?"

Sergrid's muzzle twisted in a sour grin. "*Been* there!" he laughed, "why, what do you take me for? I've not taken leave of my senses. Not yet, I haven't!"

He put a big hand to his face and scratched the red patch of skin along his jaw where fur no longer grew. The scar of an old wound, I guessed, and the mark that had earned him his name.

"To answer you fair," he said. "I've not been there and no one else has, either. Not for maybe two, three hundred years or so." He nodded darkly toward the shore and poured himself a cup of ale. "The ships that brought us here fair rotted away 'fore my father and his father was born. There's no wood for more, as you can see well enough by lookin' about. You're leaning your weight on the mast of the last of the ships there was."

He glanced fiercely at Signar-Haldring, a challenge in his eyes. "But we ain't entirely forgot where we come from, if that's what you're thinking."

"Sergrid, I was not," said Signar.

He seemed satisfied with that, and nodded to himself. "I'll tell you one thing, for certain. Even if there were ships to be had, I'd not be sailin' 'em there." He frowned, and covered the map with his hand. "It's a bad place to go. The worst there is, maybe. There's stories come down that'd curl your ears, for sure."

"What do the stories say?"

Sergrid looked down, considering his words. "The tale is, eight ships sailed to the south—and two come back."

"What happened to the others?" Signar asked.

Sergrid gave him a baleful stare. "Wouldn't any who come back *say* what they saw—or what become of the rest."

Sigmar and I were clearly waiting for more. Sergrid saw this and shook his head. "That's all there is," he said, coming to his feet. "It ought to be enough, if you got your wits about you."

"Sergrid," I asked, "did the people who came back have a name for this place? Did they call it something?"

For the first time, he looked square at me. "They called it something, all right. Though it already had a name of its own." Before I could say more, he crushed the map in his fist and thrust it roughly toward me. "You can see for yourself if you like. I've nothing more for you!"

Outside, his manner changed abruptly—as if the subject of charts to forbidding lands had never arisen. "There'll be food and good drink at the Big House on the hill," he told us. "Your folk are welcome soon as it's dark." With that he disappeared behind the heavy furs that covered his door, leaving Signar and myself alone on the chill slopes of Raadnir.

We kept to ourselves until we were well away from Sergrid's keep. Anyone who has grown up in the north knows sound carries well in the chill air.

"We did not learn a great deal," Signar said finally, "for all the time we've spent gatherin' moss on our hulls. Either that, or we got more'n we come for. I can't figure which."

"Both, most likely," I agreed. "We have a saying in the Eubirones: He who looks long enough for warts will find three more than he wanted."

Signar looked blank. "What's that supposed to mean?"

"Probably nothing. Is the chart good enough to get us there?"

"It's good enough. Take maybe fifteen, twenty days, I'd guess. Depending on winter storms and the wind. Aldair, it don't much sound like a place worth *hurryin'* to, does it?"

"No, it clearly doesn't. If it did, there'd likely be little for us to learn there. That seems to be the rule when you're deal-

ing with the blight of Man. For some reason, Signar, truth
appears to shun the earth's garden spots, preferring to hide in
cesspools."

Signar wrinkled his nose. "Is that another saying, or what?"

"No, I'm just recalling where we've been these past few
years, and where we're going next." I stopped, then, pulling
the map from my cloak and holding it to the gray light. It had
been much too dim to see the thing in Sergrid's hut, and I did
not care to wait till we reached the ship.

A good light was needed, for certain. The skin was old, and
the writing dark and faded. Most of it was in the Vikonen
tongue, which I can scarcely read. Suddenly, though, letters
I could understand jumped up as clear as rain.

"Now, that's of interest indeed!" I said, showing the spot to
Signar. "It is written plainly in Rhemian, which is close to the
language of Man. MERRKIA," I spelled. "From its position,
I'd guess it is the name of Sergrid's land to the south and west.
He *said* it had a name of its own."

"He did," Signar said grimly, "and if you'll peer beneath it,
you'll see the name his people gave it. *Rhagnir te-holna.*"

"And what does that mean?"

"*Rhagnir* is hell. *Holna* is dream. *Rhagnir te-holna* is Hell-
dream."

"Ah, well. The Vikonen are much given to exaggeration."

Signar looked pained. "Not when we put a name to a
thing, Aldair. Names are very serious to the Vikonen."

Of course, I knew this was so. Seafaring people lie about
nearly everything—but they do not jest about the ships they
sail, or the shores they touch in their ventures.

It is an act of the highest valor to attend a Vikonen feast, if
you are not of that hearty race yourself. The Big House, as it
was called by the folk of Raadnir, is in truth a great circle of
stones covered with the laced skins of countless snowdeer. This
valuable animal also furnishes fuel for the dung fires which
burn near the center of the structure. These enormous confla-
grations issue clouds of foul-smelling smoke which settle about
the room like a perpetual fog. Add to this the odor of sour ale,
dried fish and a number of unwashed giants, and you have the
general climate of such a gathering.

And of course, there is the noise. And the fighting. And the pounding of great boots upon the floor in time to some music only the Vikonen can hear.

"I have not had as much fun since we faced death in the Great Desert below Chaarduz," said Thareesh.

"You are right," I agreed, "it is an occasion of equal joy."

Rhalgorn, rigid as a rock between us, said nothing. There was blood in his eyes, and I could feel a heavy tail beating against the side of my boot. The Lords of the Lauvectii are hunters by nature; they stay alive in the northland through keen senses of smell, hearing, and near uncanny eyesight. The din about us was a terrible assault upon those faculties. More than that, what he saw and felt around him greatly affected his thinking, for the mind and the senses are closely linked in a Stygiann.

Corysia was not with us; Sergrid's sudden invitation was still not to my liking, and I wanted her safely aboard the *Ahzir*. Ordinarily, she does not like to be left behind—this time, however, she did not argue. Indeed, she would have kept the rest of us from going if she could.

The Big House was long and somewhat narrow, and as guests of Sergrid Bad-Beard we had been accorded seats of honor beside him, on a raised stone platform near one end of the room. This was some protection from the forest of hairy trees dancing and howling about. If one fell drunk to the floor —which was not uncommon—we would not be crushed to pottage.

Signar sat to my right, and beside him, Sergrid himself. Just below was a group of six or so Vikonen I had been watching for some time. One, a giant even among this gathering, had rallied those about him with some sort of banter all found greatly amusing. His humor escaped me until I suddenly realized the subject of the joke was Sergrid. Over and over, the big Vikonen grasped the fur at his muzzle and pointed to the dais. It was a crude imitation of the bare spot on Sergrid's jaw, and the gesture brought howls of laughter from the others.

I glanced quickly across Signar to Bad-Beard. Though it would be hard to miss what was happening, he seemed to take no notice at all. Signar caught my interest, and brought his head down close to mine. "I been watchin' 'em, too. It looks like trouble, if you ask me."

"Do you know who they are? They must be drunk indeed to mock him right to his face!"

"The big one's Sergrid's brother, Ghalduff. I've seen him around before. Near as I can tell from listenin' about, there's bad blood between them."

"Some of it's likely to flow," I said, "if this business goes much further."

Before Signar could speak, the laughter rose to a roar beneath us. Sergrid's brother had grabbed one of his companions and neatly flicked his knife across the fellow's muzzle. The cut was so swift and sure it never touched the skin. Ghalduff howled, and held a tuft of fur aloft, offering it to Sergrid. Again, Bad-Beard appeared not to notice. I wondered if he feared his brother, or simply held him in contempt. At any rate, Ghalduff chose that moment to drop his charade, and take up another, and I breathed a quick sight of relief. In truth, I should have known better—the festivities were just beginning.

It was all too clear what Ghalduff was about. He had called for ale, but it was the female who served it that caught his interest. He gave her a leer and said something that brought laughter from his companions. The female moved away and he grabbed her roughly to him, whispering in her ear. She jerked back, clawing his face. With an easy smile, Ghalduff cuffed her hard, sending her to the floor.

Signar sat up straight beside me, a deep growl starting in his chest. At the same time, Rhalgorn came suddenly alive. Fast as he was, Signar was faster, a dark blur leaping from the platform straight at Ghalduff's throat.

"May the gods be with us now," moaned Rhalgorn, "*that's* the large lovely fat-fur's been mooning after!"

Bruhngella. In a sudden moment of wisdom, I had guessed this. As often happens, enlightenment came too late to be of any great use.

Ghalduff was not as drunk as he seemed, for he scrambled away from Signar's death grip, and came lightly to his feet, facing his foe from a low and practiced crouch. A companion tossed him a war-axe, and found another for Signar. Signar didn't hesitate a moment. With a great roar, he leaped at Ghalduff, his axe cutting a terrible arc in the air before him.

Ghalduff backed off, startled. I could read the sudden confusion in his eyes. This was not the way one started a proper fight. First, there was a great deal of cursing and stalking about, to show one's courage. Signar, however, was not interested in formalities. He pressed Ghalduff hard, forcing him to the defensive from the beginning. Ghalduff was no amateur—but he had spent his whole life on Raadnir, and could not hope to match the battle skills of Signar-Haldring.

I knew what Signar was doing, for he had begun the fight with his right arm, which was sorely wounded in our bloody encounter on the Rhemian bridge. Ghalduff, of course, could not know this, and grew used to meeting the blade of a right-handed fighter. When Signar had him clearly trained for such an opponent, he deftly switched the weapon to his good left arm and went in for the kill.

It was not a long fight, but it had its moments. Ghalduff lasted longer than I'd expected. Then, surprise and understanding dawning on his face, he watched Signar's blade cleave him near in two from shoulder to chest.

Signar stood back, hefting his weapon for whatever might come next. I'm sure he had the same mental picture shared by Rhalgorn, Thareesh, and myself: a brief, hopeless battle that would hardly take us to the door.

The crowd, shocked for a moment by what they'd seen, suddenly came awake with a vengeance. With a great collective roar, they thundered for us across the room. Sergrid Bad-Beard came to his feet and stopped them in their tracks. Stepping down from the platform, he paused for a moment to glance at his brother, then moved to face Signar.

"This is a terrible thing you have done," he said gravely. "My brother has been slain, and though it was a fair fight, nothing will bring him to life again."

He paused, scratching his jaw, giving serious thought to the problem. Finally, he turned to face the crowd behind him. "If one of our own had drawn royal blood, he would pay with his life, for certain!" The angry Vikonen shook their fists in agreement. "As it is, these folk are guests among us, and the gods have much to say regarding their treatment." The folk of Raadnir were not overly pleased with this, but they kept their objections to themselves.

Bad-Beard turned to Signar again. "This is my sentence, Signar-Haldring of Vhiborg. You and your companions are banished from Raadnir. I would strongly advise you never to touch our shores again. And you—!" He turned, pointing an angry finger at the late Ghalduff's circle of friends. "You,

who brought my brother to this end through your foolishness
—you will take ship with them, forfeiting all titles and prop-
erties!"

Ghalduff's companions looked aghast. But Sergrid was not
finished. Glancing over the crowd, he found Bruhngella and
motioned her to him. "Child, you have suffered greatly this
day," he said gently, slipping a burly arm about her waist.
"Your mate has been slain before your eyes, and left you
homeless."

"Mate?" Signar's jaw fell open.

"However," said Sergrid, "you will not suffer more, for
the protection of the royal house is yours."

Bruhngella glanced up shyly at Sergrid, then stole a furtive
glance at the bewildered Signar.

"Now go!" thundered Bad-Beard, turning on us all, "before
wrath and sorrow overtake me!" Needing no further prod-
ding, we filed quickly out of the Big House, leaving the
angry shouts of the folk of Raadnir behind us.

Thus, we left that land on the morning tide, having finally
learned the reason we were given charts to the terrible land
called Merrkia and Hell-dream. We also gained a greater
understanding of the manner in which wise leaders rid themselves of worrisome pretenders to the throne and their companions, and how they gain property, fair maidens and the
admiration of their subjects without turning a hand in such
matters themselves.

Four

While the winds failed to speed us overnight to tropic seas, as Thareesh had hoped, the weather south was far gentler than the biting cold of Raadnir. The climate was much like the brisk days of autumn in the north of Gaullia, and all but the Nicieans among us were greatly pleased. Even Corysia admitted the weather was proper for striding about the decks, though it could not compare to the lazy days and balmy nights at the heel of the Rhemian boot.

Signar reported the water itself was warmer here, and guessed we had entered one of those broad currents which move like separate streams within the seas. Such a current runs north along the western shores of Vikonea, and is familiar to those who sail there. Rhalgorn, of course, sniffed at such a notion, declaring that water was water, and as far as he could see it simply stayed where it was, unless the wind moved it somewhere else. Signar asked him how many ships he had guided through the forests of the Lauvectii, and one thing led to another until the Stygiann was again banished forever from the bridge. This is a regular occurrence aboard the *Ahzir al'Rhaz,* and both Signar and Rhalgorn look forward to each new encounter.

Some ten days out of Raadnir we sighted land far to the starboard. We were all quite pleased at this, though Signar-Haldring merely shrugged, saying there was nothing to get excited about, since the chart of Sergrid Bad-Beard *showed* there to be land in that position—if one had a Vikonen course to follow, he could expect to see whatever there was to see. Nevertheless, I am sure he was secretly relieved.

Our six new crewmen, the exiled friends of Ghalduff, took naturally to the sea. The blood of old Vikonea ran in their veins, though they had never seen that land, nor the ships that sail from her shores. It is true they were somewhat surly at first, finding themselves far from home, among creatures they had never seen before. But they had seen Signar fight, and would not soon forget what he had done to Ghalduff. For good measure, Signar split the fellows up, dividing them equally among our three vessels.

"They'll make fine seamen," he assured me. "By the time we get where we're going, you'll scarce be able to tell 'em from the other Vikonen aboard."

"I will," I said, "because their fur is black as night, while you and every other Vikonen I know is a fair shade of cinnamon."

Signar thought about that and scratched his stomach. "I've been ponderin' on that, and think I have an answer as to why there's Vikonen on Raadnir, and how they got there. There's tales of a war fought half a thousand years ago in Norghaad-land, which is a wild and barren place east of Vhiborg. It's said that Light won over Darkness in a great battle there—like Good over Evil, you see. Only I'm not so sure the yarn ain't been twisted some—might be it was shades of fur they fought about, 'stead of somethin' else." Signar made a face and shook his head. "The way I see it, whoever *wins* some kind of fracas turns out to be the *good* side, by the time the tales get told."

"There is too much truth in what you say."

"I reckon it's the natural way of things," Signar added. "Least, it's ever been the same."

"The *natural way?*" I turned on him, angry at his words. "Natural be damned, Signar! It's the curse of Man that turns us against our kind, and breeds a hate for any creature who doesn't have a tail or a nose to match our own!"

I saw the bewilderment in his eyes, and was greatly shamed. "Signar, forgive me. The anger was not for you, old friend."

Signar shrugged his big shoulders. "I know that for a fact, Aldair, an' you're as right as rain in what you said. I reckon I'd know better'n most, wouldn't I?"

"You would indeed, for we've seen much together that neither of us cares to remember."

Storms at sea are as much a part of the sailor's life as breathing. There are no good storms—only those that are bad, and somewhat worse. The one that rushed down upon us from the south our fourteenth day at sea was strong enough to test our skills and keep us from oversleeping. Still, we had all seen winds a good deal worse. My greatest fear was that the weather might scatter our vessels far and wide, and make it difficult to come back together.

I had complete confidence in the captains of both the *Tharrin Aghiir* and the *Shamma a'Lan.* They were veteran seafarers—one a Niciean, the other a Vikonen cousin of Signar's. Each knew his craft, and carried one of the precious home-finders that is the secret of Niciean sailors—a small metal arrow that ever points to the north.

After the storm passed, the *Shamma a'Lan* was far to the east, but still in sight, and she brought her heading round quickly to match our own. Two days later, however, there was still no sign of *Tharrin Aghiir.* Even Signar-Haldring began to show concern.

"If nothing's happened to her, she ought to be findin' us sooner than this."

"It's a big sea," I told him. "Even if they're just over the horizon, they might as well be a hundred leagues away."

Signar said nothing. He turned to the bridge and sniffed the air, as if he might somehow catch the smell of *Tharrin Aghiir.* I left him there and went below, for I had in mind a way to shorten his vigil.

There are many things I remember from the haven of Man, deep beneath the great dead city on Albion Isle. There are terrors there, as well as wondrous things to behold. The pictures in the thousand ghost-gray windows that move and speak would drive a person mad if he stopped to watch them all. And while I do not countenance the works of Man, there are things I saw there that struck my fancy, and seemed to hold no harm. One was a device I would have used much sooner, had there been time and materials at hand. It would have saved us a great deal of needless searching about on our trek around the horn of Kenyarsha, when we dared not put ashore.

Thus, before we set sail across the Misty Sea, I had the device put together by craftsmen in the free Niciean port of Bhazaar, then packed aboard the *Ahzir.* My companions were much amused by the thing, especially Rhalgorn, who vowed he would cut off his own tail with Signar's war-axe if it even appeared to do what I claimed. Now, I reasoned, with the *Tharrin Aghiir* lost to our sight, I would hold him to that vow.

In truth, I was as surprised as any to see that great sphere of fabric actually *floating* a few meters off the deck, its lines all taut and secure, eager to take to the air. Perhaps, in some more sensible corner of my mind, I had imagined it would merely lie there, and do nothing at all.

"It is—somewhat larger than I thought it would be," I said, finding no other words for the moment.

"We have sayings in the Lauvectii, too," Rhalgorn said grimly. "One I recall states a person may break his neck falling out of bed, or dropping from a tree. The difference is in the time he has to think about his folly on the way down."

"That is not a saying of the Lauvectii. You made it up for the occasion."

Rhalgorn shrugged. "How do you think sayings get started? *Some*one has to be first."

"It is a fair calm day," Signar admitted. "If the rope don't break you got a chance of makin' it back."

"Thank you very much. I'll be sure to remember that."

"What happens if it leaks, Aldair?" asked Corysia. "Or if the coals go out?"

"Or if they don't," added Rhalgorn, "and set the thing afire?"

I turned and faced them, making every effort to appear a great deal calmer than I was. Thinking about such a device was one thing. Actually getting *in* it was something else again. The small reed basket at the end was looking smaller and more fragile by the minute.

"Good-bye," I said stiffly, "you may wish me a pleasant flight if you wish. As soon as I spot the *Tharrin Aghiir* I will signal to have myself pulled down again." With that, I climbed into my basket with as much dignity as I could muster.

"Just a moment," said Thareesh, jumping up beside me, "I am going too, Aldair."

I stared at him, as did all the others. "Niceans like high places, or have you forgotten?" He grinned, as well as a Nicean can do such a thing, and I grinned back, just as foolishly.

"It is good to know I have *one* brave companion!" I called to the others.

"It is sad to learn there are two fools aboard the *Ahzir*," said Signar-Haldring.

Five

———◆◆◆———

Rhalgorn was right. If one fell from such a height, he would indeed have time to contemplate his folly. While one is still aloft, however, there is much to keep him busy. The device does not just sit there, it demands a great deal of attention. There is the pan of coals to keep alive, cinders to brush away before your pants catch afire, and lines that tend to twist and tangle where they shouldn't. I was grateful for Thareesh; it is true Niceans relish high places, and enjoy such sport as hopping from one mast to another atop a ship, or hanging from the rigging by their tails.

"I imagine birds get used to this," I shouted to him over the wind, "and think nothing of it!" He nodded back, perched precariously on the edge of our basket, loosing a particularly knotty line from its companion. When he was through, he jumped down and moved closer so we could hear each other speak.

"There is one thing we did not consider in this venture, Aldair."

"Just one? I can think of several."

"I am talking about the wind," he said. "It is not the same up here as it is down there."

This was so, and the difference was most discomfiting. While the ship traveled at one speed, we proceeded at another. Thus, the rope that held us to the *Ahzir* was ever at a strain, causing our basket to tip at an alarming angle We had noticed this problem almost immediately, but hoped it would somehow go away.

"This device of yours is determined to go with the wind," Thareesh said grimly.

"I can see that. I imagined it would simply float nicely above the ship. It would be quite pleasant up here if it would do that."

30

"It would, indeed. But I do not think it intends to. I think it prefers to remain sideways."

"Thareesh, I do not think we can ignore this any longer. We are in a great deal of trouble." A strong breeze caught the inflated globe above, jerking us both off our feet and scattering hot coals about. For a moment, the Nicican's green skin turned sickly white.

"There are two things we can do," he said calmly, clutching the sides of our craft. "We can signal the ship to pull us in, which will only tip us further, or—"

"Or," I finished, "we can cut the rope and take our chances. I think we have little choice in the matter, though it is not a happy decision."

"No, it is not. But best we do something while we still have some say in the matter. Hold on, please. This is likely to be unpleasant." With that, he whipped a sharp Nicean blade from his side and loosed us from the *Ahzir*. Our basket gave a sickening lurch that nearly spilled us, then, free from all restraint, the device soared upward with dizzying speed. I risked a cautious look over the edge. There was a great deal of blue water, and little else. The *Ahzir* and *Shamma* were fast becoming small wooden chips against the sea.

"Now what?" asked Thareesh.

"Now," I said, "we have two new choices to consider. We can cover the coals and make sure no more hot air enters the device. Hopefully, we will then sink slowly back to the sea, while we are still in sight of the *Ahzir*. Or, we can achieve the same effect somewhat faster."

"I am for the faster way," Thareesh said quickly. "I think. How do we do that?"

"You climb up the lines and punch a few holes in the fabric, letting out the air."

Thareesh regarded me soberly. "I see. *I* climb up the lines."

"You are a Nicean. Niceans are good at such things."

"That's true," he nodded. "But this is a somewhat unusual height, even for Niceans. Are you aware that the birds are flying *beneath* us, Aldair?"

"I have noticed this."

"All right," sighed Thareesh, "how big a hole would you like?"

"That's the part I haven't decided yet," I explained. "If we cut too small a hole, it will do no good. On the other hand—"

Thareesh made a gesture like a rock smashing against his hand.

"Exactly," I said.

"I vote for the other way," Thareesh said glumly.

I was inclined to agree, there being no great hurry to get down to the water. Signar would follow, now that he knew what had happened to us. Under full sail, he would reach our landing spot in no time at all. Thareesh and I exchanged reassuring smiles, and covered the coals in our pan. The gentle descent would begin at any moment, I decided.

Some time later, we were still rising above the earth, moving swiftly to the west. The device seemed to care not a whit if it received additional air or not. It was doing nicely on what it had.

In one respect, we had accomplished what we set out to do. While we were hopelessly lost from two of our vessels, we were in an excellent position to spot the third. Especially if it happened to be sailing about in the direction we were going. There were times when we decided we were definitely getting lower, but it is difficult to judge such things from above the earth. Nothing gets bigger or smaller. There is the sky, the sea, and a thin line between.

"Undoubtedly," said Thareesh, "those who conceived this craft had some clever way of getting it up or down."

"It seems quite likely they did," I agreed. "It does not seem reasonable that they would climb up the lines and slash holes in the thing each time they wished to descend."

"No, it does not."

"Damn me, Thareesh! This is what comes of bringing the marvels of Man to life again. Nothing that race devised comes to good. Do you see where my dabbling has brought us. We are in a great deal of trouble, to say the least."

Thareesh sniffed the air and gave me a calm Niciean smile. "This appears to be a day for sayings, Aldair. Would you care to hear the ancient wisdom of Niciea? If one whipped himself with his tail for every sin, he would soon have only a nub."

"That's very comforting."

"Perhaps not, but it is appropriate to the moment."

"I'll tell you what's appropriate to the moment. The sun is continuing to set, as it does every day. We will soon be floating about in the dark."

Thareesh considered that. "Do you think we should make holes in the thing now, Aldair?"

"Unfortunately," I reminded him, "that is no longer one of our choices. The basket will not *float*, Thareesh. There are too many holes between the reeds. We cannot come down in that manner unless there is someone around who will pick us up very quickly."

The Niciean wrapped long fingers about his jaw. "I am ashamed to admit it, but I had not thought of that."

"Don't whip your tail to a nub over it," I said. "It will not get us down any faster, and—"

"*Aldair!* Stop mouthing wisdom and look there!"

I sat up, following his arm to the west. "What? I see nothing but the sun, and a sea bright as iron."

"There," he pointed, "on the horizon. If you had been born by the Southern Sea you could see *past* the brightness. There is a dark line there—getting darker by the moment!"

He was right, but my eyes were as heavy as lead before I could make it out. "It is either a line of rain clouds—or land."

Thareesh shook his head. "It is *not* a line of clouds," he said firmly. "And look—there are islands off to starboard."

I studied the bright scene a long moment. "They are not very large islands, if that is what they are."

"They are large enough," said Thareesh happily, "and the land is even bigger."

"It is certainly much better than landing in the sea at night," I agreed. "Now, if Signar will only—" I stopped, lifted a hand and slapped myself firmly on the forehead.

"What's that for?"

"*That* is for not thinking properly," I groaned. "We have forgotten where we are, Thareesh." What else lies to the west but Merrkia? We have come to Hell-dream, old friend."

Thareesh gave me a somber look. "Aldair, we are going to be over the place in a moment."

I leaned out, gauging our speed against the land ahead. The islands were below us, now, and we were moving swiftly toward the shore. We would be stranded on those tiny dots of stone, but it was a far better choice than Merrkia—

Thareesh grabbed my shoulder and turned me to the far side of the basket. "Aldair, I can scarcely believe my eyes," he shouted, "but it is there, for certain. Look, near that island to the left—it's the ship!"

I saw it immediately. "The *Ahzir!* How in all the hells did they get here before us!"

Thareesh shook his head. "It is not the *Ahzir*, it is the *Tharrin Aghiir*. Her mast is broken, but the crew's still aboard."

"Then they can see us!"

"Exactly." He was already halfway up the lines, snaking his way rapidly to the great fabric bag. His knife lashed out and tore a large hole in the thing. Then another. And another.

"Thareesh," I yelled, "damn it all, that's enough!"

The wind carried my words away and the Niciean went about his work with a vengeance. He had waited long enough to bring this craft to ground, and he was determined to do the job right.

Suffice it to say we did not fall gently to the sea. The bag collapsed of a sudden and we plummeted to earth like a stone. One moment we soared majestically as a hawk—the next, we had all the grace and beauty of a sack of turnips.

I recall many things about the trip down. Most memorable was the sight of Thareesh, a green blur of arms, legs, and tail attempting to climb back into the air on nothing more substantial than a loose strand of rope. There was a very startled expression on his face when he came to the end of this fragment.

Six

Though one seldom gets credit for his achievements, he is nearly always recognized for his mistakes. This is probably a saying in some land or other. If it isn't, it should be.

Our companions were both surprised and relieved to find us alive and reasonably well, waiting for them aboard the crippled *Aghiir*. There followed a happy reunion, and the quaffing of a fair amount of ale and barley beer. Following that was a near endless round of comments regarding our venture:

Rhalgorn: Signar, what's that soaring high up there against the sun? I'd say it was a hawk, but it is faster, and far less graceful. An owl, perhaps?

Signar: Can't be an owl, it's got a curly tail and one ear . . .

Rhalgorn: By the gods, I know it now—it's the rare short-snouted flying Veniciil

Signar: Damn me, I think you're right. And look—there's another, all green and scaly-like. A whip-tailed Niciean bug-catcher, for certain!

I will mention only one of these droll bits of conversation; they were all of the same cloth, and wore thin rather quickly, to my way of thinking.

Corysia was not amused by my soaring venture. To her, it seemed a needless bit of folly, though I pointed out that we had, in a manner of speaking, found the *Aghiir*. This was undoubtedly the wrong thing to say, for she immediately stormed off to our cabin and stayed there for some time. At least, I had the sense not to tell her the flying device had been

retrieved from the sea, and was even now being repaired for
future use. Thareesh and I had already devised several ways
in which the thing might be improved, and better controlled.
As I say, this was hardly the time to discuss such matters with
Corysia.

Before noon, I met with Signar-Haldring and his captains
to take stock of our situation. All three agreed that the land
before us was indeed the one called Merrkia on Sergrid's
chart. However, they were not at all sure we were anywhere
near the spot the expedition from Raadnir had gone ashore.
Signar believed it was somewhat to the south. Bhaldrig and
Seeshar felt it was probably to the north. We could sail off
in several directions in an effort to pinpoint the location, but
there was little merit in that. I did not relish the idea of leaving
the *Aghiir* alone on a strange shore, without a proper mast.

"You ask me," Signar said grimly, "one landin' is as good
or bad as another, if the tales be true about this place. Trouble's likely to find us, even if we're a point or two off course."

"That's a cheering thought," I told him, "and you're probably right as rain. Still, I'd like to come as close as we can.
I think it's important that we find—whatever it is the others
found."

Seeshar reached down to bring the chart closer to his eyes.
He was old, but able. His green skin was parched by years of
service to an empire and a king he had now outlasted.

"Aldair," he said, "it is my guess we could come ashore at
the place we seek a hundred times or more—and still not
know for certain we were there. All lands look alike in one
respect; they've bays and coves and beaches by the thousands,
and one's much like another. 'Less there's something there to
guide you, or it's a place you've been before, there's no true
way to say you've come to where you want."

Signar and Bhaldrig nodded agreement. I looked beyond
them, at the small islands to starboard. Farther, a low mist
hugged the shore, shrouding the land of Merrkia. "Then that's
the way it'll be," I told them. "We'll sail as one, and search
the coast for a likely landing. It may take a little longer this
way, but we'll all rest easier knowing there're two ships beside us."

"If there is truth in the tales of Raadnir," Seeshar added,
"it would be most prudent to face such a land together."

Thus, at dawn the next day, the *Ahzir* and *Shamma al'Lan*

pointed their bows to the mainland, the *Aghiir* in tow. The
sun shone brightly and a crisp breeze blew in for the asking
to fill our sails. Even the coast of Merrkia seemed green and
inviting. The waters here were surprisingly gentle, with little
movement below the surface. This is not always the way
close to shore, where hidden currents can prove quite treacherous. Signar said the many small islands paralleling the
shore acted as a protective reef against the sea.

I was somewhat curious about these islands, which looked
like none I had seen before. Few were overly large, and one
seemed much like another—bare, rocky hummocks that
scarcely topped the surface. As we came closer to the land
they seemed to get somewhat higher, but none rose more
than a few meters above the sea. Signar could not explain
these phenomena, nor could any of the veteran seamen aboard
the *Ahzir*. Each, however, noted that there is ever something
new in the world.

While I weighed these words of wisdom, someone touched
me lightly on the arm and I turned to see Corysia. She said
nothing, but merely stood beside me watching our bow churn
the sea to foam.

"It is a sight that always makes me thirsty," I said, nodding
at the frothy water, "for it looks a great deal like the head
on a fine mug of ale."

"That is not an overly colorful allusion," Corysia said
coolly.

"There is nothing overly colorful about a mug of ale, but
it is a nice thing to think about. Of course, sometimes the
sea is a different shade, and I am reminded of the froth on
a cup of strong barley beer, which is somewhat thicker and—"

"*A*ldair . . ."

I grinned at her, and she raised her snout and looked away.
"I am still not speaking to you."

"You just did."

"I forgot."

"Good."

"But now I have remembered."

"If it is still that business of the soaring device—"

"That is exactly what it is."

"Corysia," I said, turning her around to face me, "what
more is there to say on the subject?"

"Perhaps nothing. But I am—still thinking about it."

"Then think about something else."

"Such as?"

"Well, we could explore the subject of colorful allusions."

"I am not in the mood for allusions."

"Well, then—"

"Aldair, you might have been killed."

"But I wasn't."

She sighed, brushing a bit of spray from her fine auburn hair. "Will you promise me something, Aldair?"

"What's that?" I knew, of course, exactly what it was.

"That you will never, *ever* do such a foolish thing again!"

I have always found it difficult to stretch the truth when Corysia is looking me straight in the eye. "There is one thing I will promise you," I said as solemnly as possible, "here and now, Corysia. . . ."

"Aldair!" Signar bellowed my name from the bridge.

"Corysia, I have to go."

"But you haven't—!"

"I know. But I will." I turned, and hurried quickly for the bridge, silently thanking whatever gods had chosen to pull me out of the fire at a most appropriate moment.

Signar pointed to the shore. "It's the mouth of a river, and from the look of it, fair deep enough to take our hulls. We could make a better port there, Aldair, an' still have clear water at our backs."

It was indeed a worthy idea, and I quickly agreed. We could not say what we might face in this land, and a fast way to leave it was much to my liking. Signar shouted a command, and the *Ahzir al'Rhaz* veered hard to starboard, great sails whipping in the wind. The mouth of the river opened blue and wide before us.

I found it interesting that the small islands off Merrkia did not stop at the shore, but continued up the river itself, finally becoming tangled in foliage along the banks on either side. For nearly a full minute, I stood by the railing and watched this sight, enjoying the view. Then, slowly, it dawned on me that there was something drastically wrong with such reasoning. Islands did *not* march upriver and line themselves up along its banks! Indeed, they did nothing of the sort!

With sudden clarity, I realized exactly what I was seeing.

And with understanding, came the proverbial chill at the back of my neck. These were not islands at all, but stunted towers of old. Our river was not truly a river, but a broad avenue over a sunken city of Man.

Seven

The ruins of Man can be seen in every land, though few recognize them for what they are. The farmer who breaks his plow on the roots of a long-dead city may curse the stones that block his way—but he will not question how they came to be there. There are cities now, are there not? In stands to reason there were cities in the past.

The priests and scholars of every race have much the same story to tell: History began some three thousand years ago. All that has happened lies within that time, from the first day of the world, till now. The myths of creation vary little from one land to another. My people say the creatures of the earth first appeared in Albion, where they sinned against the Creator, and were cast out upon the world. The Vikonen tell the story in a different manner, as do the Nicieans. Each, however, include the Dark Isle of Albion in their tale. They are right to do so, but not for the reasons they imagine. I have been to Albion, and I know its terrible secret. There, indeed, is where we began—but the rest of the story is a lie. The sin is Man's, not ours, for it was he who fashioned us from beasts to mirror his own sad history.

Why did he do this thing? That, I cannot say. Perhaps he gained some pleasure watching the shame and glory of his race relived again.

Whatever the sin of Man, there is no denying the marvels of his world. We had sailed the broad river near half a day, and there was still no end to the city. On either side, as far as the eye could see, pale fingers the color of ash crowded one upon another. The forest had long since returned to claim its own, but one could imagine how it might have been. I do not think the years could ever cover its glory.

The crew of the *Aghir* is normally a noisy lot. Sailors like

40

to talk and sing as they work, or call out some obscenity to a friend. Now, they neither sang nor spoke to one another. The awesome quiet of the land touched every creature aboard. I think they sensed the ghosts of Man around them, and knew they beheld a sight they were never meant to see. There was a fear and wonder here they could neither name nor fathom, and this was mirrored in their faces.

The size of the city was truly beyond belief. At every turn of the river we expected to see its ending. Even such a place as this, we reasoned, could not go on forever.

"It's all the cities in the world put together," said Signar-Haldring, "and then some. What d'you reckon made 'em want to get all bunched up together, Aldair? It don't seem like such a fine idea to me."

"I used to ask myself the same question when I was in Silium, at the University," I told him. "The town certainly seemed big enough to me, though I imagine you could put everyone there in one of these towers when it stood, and still have room for the folk of Camelium and Culvia. In all honesty, I cannot answer your question."

"Well, it don't make much sense, as I see it," he growled, and scratched his broad back against the mast.

"Perhaps it did to those who lived here," I reminded him. "The moving windows under Albion pictured machines that moved swiftly through the air and over the ground. It did not take overly long to get from one place to another."

"What's the big hurry to get somewhere else," he said, sweeping a broad hand across the horizon, "if it's just like the place you left behind?"

I could argue that. I have never understood why creatures wish to crowd themselves together in narrow streets that shut out the sun. Yet, many of them do, and become lonely without the stink of their neighbors. Clearly, even Man was not immune to such folly. . . .

As near as I could guess, the structure had fallen in upon itself over the ages. Two great walls had held, catching the fill from the rest of the building. This debris formed a hill that even my short legs could manage. Rhalgorn, of course, bounded ahead, stopping now and then to grin down inanely and start small showers of dirt and stone in my direction. At twenty meters, our perch gave a fine view of the surrounding

territory. Though we had passed taller structures on the river,
this was by far the loftiest in the neighborhood. None
matched the towers of the Avakhar, which still reach twenty
stories or more in magnificent ruin, but I was certain there
had been such buildings here.

"Now that we have reached the top of this thing, what are
we supposed to do?" Rhalgorn asked irritably.

"We are supposed to look about us, and see what we can
see," I told him. "I assume your much-touted eyesight will
serve us well."

Rhalgorn sniffed and looked away. "The keen vision of the
Lords of the Lauvectii is no joking matter, Aldair. On a clear
day such as this—"

"I know. You can count the lice on a circling hawk."

Rhalgorn looked surprised. "I have mentioned this before?"

"Once or twice. Only we are not looking for lice today."

"I am aware of what we are looking for. We are looking
for possible danger, and as far as I can tell, there is none
about at the present."

"Good."

"There is, however, a green bottle fly perched about two
meters below the top of our mast."

I ignored this, and peered down the slope of our lookout to
the river. The *Ahzir* and her sister ships were anchored in
midstream a good quarter-league away. On the shore, behind
a formidable barrier of stone, I had set up our camp, with a
perimeter of sentries posted on high points about the area.
While it was still light, three well-armed scouting parties pa-
trolled just outside the circle of our sentries. Such precautions
were no guarantee against danger, but they would prevent us
from being taken by surprise, if anything was out there. It
had not been necessary to caution the crew against wandering
aimlessly about. Though the folk of Raadnir had met disaster
here over three centuries ago, they had not forgotten where
we were.

"That bottle fly," I said, "the one on the mast. What color
are its eyes?"

Rhalgorn's red tongue flicked out and licked his muzzle.
"Black," he answered, without a moment's hesitation. "With
just a touch of yellow."

By the time we reached camp, two of our scouting parties

had returned. Neither had seen anything of note besides birds, hares, and squirrels. There were, however, droppings among the ruins which indicated the presence of something bigger.

"How *much* bigger?" Rhalgorn wanted to know. Big enough, the scout reported, though he could not say what had made them.

"I don't care for the sound of that," I told Rhalgorn.

The Stygiann shrugged. "Just because they are large does not mean they are dangerous." His voice told me he was not entirely convinced of this.

"Sergrid's ancestors did not call this land Hell-dream for nothing," I reminded him, and instructed our scouts to tell the sentries what we knew, and to set up another line of guards just inside our outer ring. I was about to send word to Signar aboard the *Ahzir,* when something crashed heavily through the brush behind us. Every soul in the camp went for his weapons, then relaxed as a big Vikonen appeared out of the greenery. He stopped in his tracks, staring at us wide-eyed.

"What is it? What's wrong!" I asked him.

"Thareesh . . . Master Thareesh. . . ."

"Thareesh *what,* damn you!" shouted Rhalgorn.

The poor fellow was too frightened to speak. All he could do was point dumbly in the right direction. With a sudden chill, I remembered Thareesh led our third party of scouts. As one, Rhalgorn and I raised our weapons and plunged through the forest, half the camp behind us.

Eight

I cannot say what I expected to find when we reached
Thareesh. And though I conjured every possible sort of demon in my mind, I was not prepared for the thing that faced
us—the ultimate demon himself. For that, indeed, is what
Thareesh had discovered. And though it was only the demon's
image, it was no less frightening to behold.

There was a small clearing, in the shadow of great oaks. In
the center of this clearing was an awesome statue, carved of
pale white marble. It was remarkably intact, considering the
ages it had stood there. Bits and pieces had been worn away
by countless days of sun and rain, but there was no mistaking
what it was. The face of Man looked down upon us from the
past, a touch of eternal scorn at the corner of his mouth,
pride in his empty stone eyes. He was naked, except for a
length of cloth laid across his shoulder and over the crook of
his arm. The image was so finely crafted, even the muscles
and veins were well defined.

Thareesh and two Niciean crewmen stood before the thing,
near rigid under its gaze. Those who had followed me from
the camp seemed unable to move or speak. I was filled with
shame and anger—yet, I nearly laughed aloud at the pitiful
sight. An oaken glen and a terrible idol of stone—what a perfect spot for poor dumb creatures to worship their god!

I jerked a coil of line from my belt and turned about to
find the Vikonen who'd brought us there. Before he could
move, I lashed the line sharply across his face as hard as
I could. He stumbled back, startled.

"*You,*" I told him, "get a rope around that thing and bring
it down!"

He stared at me, total disbelief etched across his features.
I whipped the blade from my belt and brought it up hard
against his belly. "Now, damn you—do it. Or I'll spill your

fat gut right here. You are a Vikonen warrior—you do not squat in fear like a hare before a piece of stone!"

For an instant, I thought he might pick me up in one big fist and squeeze me into porridge. Then, blood came to his eyes and a deep growl started in his chest. The coil snaked out and caught the statute about its shoulders. A terrible battle cry rang from the Vikonen's throat and shook the quiet glen.

The spell was broken. Every creature then joined in, venting their shame against the image of Man. Those who had no ropes about them lent their arms to those who did. A warrior of Raadnir leaped atop the statute and wrapped two burly arms about its head. With a mighty roar, he sent it tumbling to the ground. His feat brought cheers from the others, and a moment later, the idol cracked at the waist and fell to earth. The marble, brittle from the years, shattered in a thousand pieces.

But they were not yet finished. Not a being there stopped his work until every fragment was reduced to shreds of stone. When they were through, and turned to face me, I saw no fear in their eyes.

"Make certain every member of the crew is brought to this place," I told them. "For I would have them see the image of Man."

During the next few days the camp fell into a regular routine of work. I had picked four scouting parties whose sole duties were exploration and discovery. These were captained by Corysia, Thareesh, and two crewmen who had shown some skill at poking about ancient places. Certainly, we could not hope to mount a full-scale archaeological expedition on the shores of Merrkia. Unearthing the secrets of one or two structures would be a lifetime task for a larger party than ours. My instructions were to pick up artifacts of interest from those areas that were accessible, or appeared safe to explore.

From my experience on Albion, and in the land of the Avakhar, I had learned that the true ground levels of ancient cities lay somewhat below the present surface. While this makes exploration extremely difficult without a great deal of digging, it also poses certain advantages: What time destroys, it can also protect. Thus, the erosion of the ages will sometimes seal pockets of treasure and leave them virtually untouched. These were the places we were looking for. We would find things of little value, I knew, and things whose purpose we could not begin to comprehend. But if we found even one small item that gave us further knowledge of the treachery of Man, we could count our mission successful.

In the next eight days, my crews found safe passage below the earth in five separate areas. These entries led to the discovery of a number of different rooms, shops, and hallways containing ancient artifacts. Many were aged beyond recognition; others turned to dust at the touch. I list here only a few of the more noteworthy finds discovered intact:

● A shop containing enough exquisite dishes, cups, glassware and cooking utensils to set table for a small army.

● A number of large rooms, mostly in ruin, containing row after row of shiny metal tables, largely rusted away. Upon each table were the remains of some incomprehensible device. The metal parts of these devices were also badly corroded, but there was another material present which had stood the test of the ages—a hard, glasslike substance which felt slick as river pebbles to the touch. For the most part, this material was found in the form of button-sized wafers imprinted with a single letter of the alphabet. There were many roomsful of of these desks and devices, but we could not fathom their purpose.

● A great many coins of silver, copper, and other metals.

● Bottles of all sizes, shapes and colors.

● A shop which held thousands of devices made of two round pieces of glass held together by a material much like that described above. We immediately guessed what these were for. When one peered through them, things seemed to become larger, so we

knew they must be akin to the spyglasses used by
ships' captains. Some of these devices, however, did
not improve the vision at all, but made it worse.
Many contained glass which made the world seem
green, blue, or yellow—a property which seemed
fairly useless.

• A clear block of glass-like material with several
shiny coins imbedded inside.

• A small statue of a creature which looked somewhat like a mouse. It had black ears, a white face and
red pants. There were white gloves on its hands and
yellow shoes on its feet. We decided it was probably a
minor deity of some sort.

• A broken glass, with a single fly imbedded in petri-
fied liquid at its base.

• The remains of a mechanical clock, much like the
intricate devices I had seen in the court of Niciea.
These, however, were infinitely more complex.

One of the most interesting finds was a paper booklet,
completely intact. It had been sealed against the air in some
transparent material which miraculously protected it through
the ages. I cannot say how the pictures in this booklet were
formed; however, since there were words there as well, I
can only imagine Man devised some wondrous form of printing far beyond our own. The subjects of these pictures were
male and female members of the race of Man in an infinite
variety of mating positions. Our crew had been in high spirits
since the destruction of the statue in the glen. After I passed
this booklet among them, whatever awe or respect they still
harbored for their "god" dissolved in gales of laughter.

I have seen pictures of Men before, in the great halls below
Albion. They are ugly creatures, with little pinched faces
and near shapeless blobs where a muzzle or snout should be.
Their tiny ears lay flat against their skulls, and their bodies
appear freshly shorn of every tuft of hair or fur. Still, when
I first viewed this creature, I thought he was surely a most

fearsome Lord of the Earth, for he built great cities and was full of awesome powers.

For all of that, he does not appear too lordly in the pages I passed among my companions. As I see it, his ruttings are not overly different from those of the beings he created.

Nine

"If there's some key to the mind of Man in all this, I sure ain't seen it yet," groaned Signar. He rubbed a small artifact between his big fingers, turning it first one way, then the other. Finally, he shrugged and tossed it aside. The Vikonen was clearly uncomfortable, for there was little room to move about. The small corner we'd picked to store our finds was now full to overflowing.

"I don't think we should expect to unearth anything of great interest," said Thareesh. "The place is much too vast for that—we knew this in the beginning."

"There's the booklet," I said. "Surely you consider that important, Thareesh." The Niciean gave me a very dubious look. Signar snorted in disgust.

"I am quite serious," I assured them. "To my way of thinking, our finds have taught us a good deal about Man. If nothing else, we have surely stripped him of his godhood. He was a creature who knew a great deal more about the mysteries of the world than we do. But knowledge is not the same as wisdom. It is clear he had no qualms about abusing his wondrous powers."

"There ain't much question about that," growled Signar.

"And I think you will both agree that what we have *not* found here is most significant, to say the least."

Signar nodded silent understanding. "The Man-thing," said Thareesh.

"Exactly. We have not talked a great deal about it, for there was little need to. It has been in all our minds from the beginning—since we learned what Sergrid's ancestors called this land. If Hell-Dream is not a fitting description of the fate of Rhemia, I would like to hear one better. I don't imagine one among us would have been surprised to find those terrible devices here, as well."

49

"I can't say I'm greatly disappointed we was wrong," Signar said dryly.

"Were we, though?" said Thareesh. "Just because we have not found them doesn't mean they aren't here."

"In a way, I think it does," I told him. Remember, this was Man's own city, where he lived and worked and took his pleasure. Why would he store such a terrible device in a place like this? We know what happens when something goes wrong."

"Rhemia," said Thareesh.

"Right. It is not the kind of thing one keeps in the cellar."

Signar rose, stretched his great frame and came around to fill his cup. "If it's not the kind of Hell-Dream we were thinkin' about, what kind is it, Aldair? *Something* happened to the folk of Raadnir. Vikonens will spin a fine yarn, and I'll grant you we might stretch the truth at times—but Bad-Beard's people come to Merrkia, and that's a fact. And wasn't many of 'em ever left the place alive."

Of course, this was a question I couldn't answer. I would have given much to know the solution to that particular mystery, and another that plagued my mind as well: *Why did Man build the greatest city in the world—then abandon it forever?*

In the Eubirones where I was born, mothers tell their children the night is the dream of the day. In many ways, I suppose this is true. Shapes and colors most familiar hide their faces after dark, and will not let us see them as they are. In this manner, the night cloaks ugliness and beauty with equal ease.

Under a full moon, the city of Man lost much of its awesome power and seemed a pleasant place to be. Silver marked the river, and I could see the masts of our ships against the sky. Even the gaunt ruins took on a soft and pearly hue. Past the riverfront and through the familiar paths of our campsite, I moved into the deeper shadow of oaks and maples. Just beyond was our first sentry. I stopped to let him know I'd be about, and that I would be grateful if he did not lose an arrow in my direction.

A few meters past him the real forest began. Heavy branches formed a near solid roof overhead, and even the bright cast of the moon was lost to view. I moved cautiously here, stopping now and again to listen to the night. Ahead, the trees thinned briefly where a narrow stream coursed by in silence. Beyond the stream was a low stone wall, rounded by the ages and ribboned in pale light and shadow. I studied this scene a long moment, letting my eyes touch every leaf and patch of earth. Finally, certain nothing was there, I took a careful step into the clearing. As my boot touched the ground, a shadow peeled itself from nowhere and moved in my direction.

To my credit, I did not leap out of my skin, but merely froze in my tracks, making a fine target.

"That was not bad," said Rhalgorn. "It appears I have taught you a little about the forest, though not a great deal."

"I was extremely silent," I told him. "You would never admit it, but I am near certain you had no idea I was there."

"Creator's Eyes, I *said* it was well done. You made no more noise than a small horse."

"Thank you. I'm sure that is some kind of compliment."

"You may take it as such, if you like," he sniffed.

I dropped down beside him near the stream, my back against the stone wall. "We missed you at supper. You have been making yourself scarce."

Rhalgorn didn't answer.

"Corysia has asked about you. Several times."

I glanced at him in the near darkness. Red eyes pierced the night, and his long muzzle twitched in the frosty air. He could not see lice on a hawk, or flies atop our mast, but little else missed his attention. At the moment, I am sure there was scarcely a sight, smell, or sound within half a league that escaped his keen senses. Stygianns are cunning and deadly creatures under any circumstances—in the depths of the forest they have no equal. I would know this better than most, for clan Venicii has fought the Lords of the Lauvectii as long as anyone can remember. Until Rhalgorn's kinsman Rheif and I were thrown together by mutual ill fortune, I'd wager not two friendly words had passed between our races.

Thus, I knew this fellow as well as any creature can, and at the moment I was certain he was deeply troubled. A Stygiann's features may tell you nothing, but the twitching of his tail speaks volumes.

"Rhalgorn," I said finally, "your thoughts are dark enough

to choke the night. I'd as soon hear what they are as wonder at them."

Rhalgorn shrugged. "Perhaps I am thinking about hares. It is a pleasant subject to contemplate."

"You are not thinking about hares."

"No?"

"No. You usually are, but this time you are not."

Rhalgorn sighed. "You're right, I'm not."

"What, then?" Rhalgorn didn't answer. Instead, he rose silently to his feet and stalked to the edge of the clearing. He stood there a long moment, gazing into the woods beyond. When he returned, there was a different look about his eyes. And when he spoke, he did not quite face me.

"Aldair," he said thoughtfully, "much has happened to me since we met at the edge of the Lauvectii and I took up the sword of my kinsman. In many ways, I am not the same as I was before. I have sailed over water, which is an unbelievable act for a Stygiann. Stranger still, I have become companion to other creatures, and learned to see some good in them. Even Signar fat-fur. Though if you ever tell him such a thing, I will remove your other ear."

He paused, scratching his pelt fiercely, as if the proper words might be buried there. "I share your quest, Aldair. I have learned a deep hatred for Man. Blood-thoughts come to my head when I think of the terrible thing he has done to us all. In this, I am of one mind with you, and Thareesh and the others. In some ways, though, I am not like any of you."

"We can share a single goal," I said, "without being the same."

"No," Rhalgorn shook his head impatiently. "That is not what I am saying. I am telling you I look at the *world* in a different way, Aldair. All Stygianns do. I see your need to explore the cities of Man. To search for clues to his treachery. But *I* do not look to cities for answers. Such places are alien to the Lords of the Lauvectii. We do not build them ourselves —moreover, we have no liking for those who do."

"This is a thing I understand," I told him.

"In some ways you do," he said. "In others, you do not. I will tell you this, Aldair—" He turned to face me squarely. "There are smells, here, and sounds—and things that can be seen and yet not seen. And they have nothing to do with this great garbage dump of Man."

"What kinds of things?"

"I cannot say. I only know that they are here. Stygianns are closer to the earth than other races—I did not fully understand the meaning of this until I met creatures that were not the same as I. Aldair—" He stopped, searching for words. "I must tell you that I have had a god-dream."

I nodded, but said nothing.

"Ordinarily, a Stygiann does not speak of such a thing to others, but I know you have some knowledge in these matters. You have told me of the being who came to you in the Great Desert—the one who set you on your quest, and guides you still."

"Sometimes I believe this," I told him. "At others, I am sure I am no more than a fool, guided by nothing at all."

Rhalgorn looked appalled. "It is neither seemly nor wise to say such things!"

"You are probably right. Now, tell me your god-dream. I am aware of this talent of the Stygianns, and I assure you I would neither scorn such a thing, nor take it lightly."

Rhalgorn gave me a weary smile. "Talent or curse, I am not sure which comes closer to the mark. And I am certain you will not take it lightly, once you hear it. The dream has come to me more than once, Aldair. I see us all, here in the ruined city of Man. I see us fall upon our own kind—and devour ourselves."

"*What?*" Something cold touched my chest, and it had little to do with the chill night air. "Rhalgorn, I mean no disrespect to your god-dream, but I do not understand this. Surely you don't believe we are going to do any such thing."

"I believe nothing," he said flatly. "All I can tell you is what I saw in the dream. Each devours his own kind. The worst that is in us all comes from the shadows, and we turn upon ourselves."

"And you can say no more?"

"Aldair, there is nothing more I *know*. . . ."

Stygianns rarely take others into their confidence. When they do, I have noticed, it is usually for some less than pleasant reason. Certainly, I could not credit Rhalgorn's god-dream. But I could not forget it, either. *Devour ourselves?* Was that the meaning of Hell-Dream—the thing the folk of Raadnir could not bring themselves to say? If that was so, one could hardly blame them. But what could make them do such a thing—*turn on their own kind?*

Needless to say, sleep did not come easily that night. When it did, I would have given much to be awake again, tossing and turning about.

Just before dawn, Corysia shook me awake and sent me to the door of our quarters. Signar, Rhalgorn, and Thareesh were waiting for me, and it was easy to tell they did not bring pleasant news. Two of our sentries were missing. There was no sign that anything had happened to them—they had simply vanished from sight.

Ten

Seasoned warriors learn to adapt themselves to nearly any hardship. They can fight under the blazing sun, or in the terrible throes of winter. They can sleep while a battle rages about them, and eat food they would normally find disgusting. A good soldier has a fair chance of surviving such a life. He is in far greater danger when he has a comfortable campsite by a river, good food and light duty. Since he sees no enemies about, he soon forgets that they exist. Shortly after he begins to reason in this manner, he discovers he is dead.

Less than a quarter hour after we learned our sentries were missing, the camp was abandoned and all our goods moved back to the vessels. Signar ordered our ships to the center of the river, and speeded up work on the new mast and rigging for the *Aghiir*. Certainly, there would be no more scouting about for artifacts. I gave hurried instructions to load a few of the more interesting pieces aboard the *Ahzir*, and left the others where they lay.

Once again, our crew looked like the warriors they were. Each was armed to the teeth, and wore helms and full armor. There was blood in their eyes, and grim determination in their features. They did not know what they might face this morning, but I saw no fear in any creature. There is a peculiar thing about donning weapons and armor. One feels he has suddenly been cloaked in a near mystical aura of invulnerability—that while a blade might fell his companion, he cannot be touched himself. If you are a warrior by trade, it is best to believe this.

There was a chill to the day, and gray clouds scudded close to the earth. The air was damp and full of the promise of rain—truly a morning to fit the mood of our company. Ahead, the line of tumbled ruins we had been following suddenly gave way to a dense grove of trees. Rhalgorn signaled a halt and went to his knees to search the ground. I left our party and went to meet him.

"Anything?"

"Something," he muttered, "but I am not sure what. The earth here is too hard to take tracks." Crouching until his muzzle near touched the ground, he brushed the soil aside with his fingers, then snapped a twist of dry grass and brought it to his nose.

"What is it?"

"I do not know, Aldair." A deep frown crossed his brow. He gave me a peculiar, searching look, then stood and shook his head. "It is a strange odor. Familiar, yet not at all."

"That doesn't tell us much."

"It tells *me* a great deal," he said solemnly. "We are quite close to *some*thing, and whatever it is, it is not to my liking." He sniffed the air, first one way and then another. "This way," he said finally, "and have your people take a care, Aldair."

The Stygiann led us quietly through the trees and into another small clearing. There were more ruins here, the shell of some great structure. Thick-walled, and made of sturdy gray Man-stone, it had stood the ravages of time rather well, holding off the strangling foliage that had threatened to bring it down over the ages. The wall we followed was nearly five meters high in places, and seemed to stretch on forever. We moved along its base, keeping the safety of solid stone at our backs, and a keen eye on the dense undergrowth beside us. In one respect, it was a sound way to travel, for there were fewer directions from which danger could threaten. Still, if anything *did* approach us from the forest, or the narrow pathway ahead and behind, we could bring only a small part of our force to bear against it. I said nothing to Rhalgorn, but I was most anxious to be out of the place.

Rhalgorn stopped a number of times to test the air, and carefully study the path ahead. Finally, I called a halt to let our warriors have a swallow of water or a bite of whatever they'd brought in their sacks. This did not last long, for they were not overly anxious to linger there. Before we started out again I moved up ahead to speak to Rhalgorn. The way ahead seemed to have no ending, and the forest was growing thicker by the moment. I wondered how long he intended to keep us

on this path. He saw me, and started to speak—then his head
jerked quickly to one side and he froze in his boots. Waving
me back, he took a cautious step forward. Then another. I
saw what he was about. There was a patch of shadow against
the wall ahead, a wide cleft where the stone had given way.
The Stygiann inched his way to the opening, dropped one
hand to the hilt of his sword, and peered inside.

It happened in the blink of an eye. One moment Rhalgorn
was planted solidly on the earth; the next, he was a gray blur
of motion in the air. Something large and ugly burst through
the hole, scattering stone and mortar across its back. With a
terrible roar, it came straight for me. I clawed up the sheer
wall like a great bug, grasping every bit of vine and foliage
in sight.

The awesome beast passed beneath me, brushing my boots
with its hide. Behind it, a veritable flood of the creatures
erupted from the dark hole and thundered down the narrow
way. Above the din of their passage I could hear the shouts
and cries of my warriors.

This whole scene lasted seconds at the most, but it seemed
a good deal longer. I dropped to the ground and ran back
along the path—Rhalgorn was already there. Our warriors
were somewhat shaken, but none seemed the worse for wear.
They were gathered about something in the grass at the
edge of the forest. I already knew what it was.

Rhalgorn stood in my way. I looked at him. "You knew,
didn't you? Back past the grove, when you sniffed the ground."

"I guessed, Aldair. I didn't know."

"You stared at me in a peculiar manner."

Rhalgorn looked at something else. "Perhaps I did." I moved
past him, and the others made room for me. The Vikonen
who had felled the thing saw me coming. He dropped his
bloody war-axe and turned away.

This was not the first time I had looked upon my ancestor.
They are all there to see below Albion, in cages of glass—the
beasts Man used to fashion his creatures. One is a great
shaggy animal beside a rushing stream. He is pawing a
silvery fish from the water. Another cage shows two gaunt
beasts at the edge of a wintry forest. One tears at his kill,
while the other raises its muzzle to the moon. There are small
green creatures with long tails and scaly hides, basking in the

sun. And there are ancestors of the Tarconii, and the Kenyashii, and the folk of Avakhar.

Finally, there are fat, round-bodied animals with short, hooved feet and curly tails. They have long snouts and flappy ears and bristles on their chins. One munches dried corn beside a fence. Another, a female, suckles her young.

There are names for these beasts, inscribed below their cages. But they do not say Vikonen or Stygiann or Niciean. My own noble forebears are called neither Rhemian nor Gaullian nor Eubirones. Animals who grovel in the mud need no such names as these.

I looked at the thing lying there in its death-blood, then turned and walked away. I did not wish to face the others in the presence of the beast.

We found our two sentries beyond the wall, or what remained of them, which was nothing we cared to gaze at very long. Gruesome bits and pieces were scattered over a wide area, mixed with the droppings of the creatures. It would have been near impossible to bury them, and it was not a task I'd ask of their companions. The best thing for us was to leave this place, and the sooner the better.

I found Rhalgorn on the far side of the structure. He was squatting on his haunches, studying the ground. "I am getting the crew together," I told him. "We have found what we came for, and then some." Rhalgorn didn't answer.

"What are you doing there?"

"Looking for something."

"What?"

"You will know when I find it!" he snapped irritably. I stood there a moment, watching his backside, then left to get the crew in order. There is no use talking to a Stygiann when he doesn't wish to talk. And we were all entitled to be a little touchy, I supposed. At the moment, I did not feel overly friendly myself. It was not exactly the setting for companionship and barley beer.

I did not have to urge our party to begin the trek back home. They were eager to leave that terrible sight behind them, and start for the river. They did not talk among themselves, or trade bawdy jokes, as warriors sometimes do after a battle. Instead, they placed one boot stolidly ahead of the other, and kept their silence.

We came at last to the end of the long wall, and headed for the grove beyond. I had not seen Rhalgorn on the march, but thought little of it. No doubt, he was bringing up the rear, still sulking to himself. Then, I heard the warriors muttering behind me and turned to see him, racing toward the head of the column as fast as he could. I stared at him, taken aback, for he was fighting for breath and pale as ash. "Rhalgorn—"

"No," he rasped, "there is no time for talk. Just listen." He jerked me off the path, away from the others. "Say nothing to them. Just . . . get them back to the ship . . . run them all the way if you have to."

"Rhalgorn, what—"

"Aldair," he groaned, "you will kill us all with questions! Here!" He thrust his fist under my chin and opened it. In his palm was a tuft of bloody gray fur.

I looked at him. "What is it?"

He bared his teeth and took a deep breath. "Those creatures did *not* kill our sentries and drag them to the wall, Aldair. They merely finished the leavings. If you think your ancestors are frightening, wait till you see *mine*—and you will, by all the gods, if we stand here talking much longer!"

Eleven

Luckily, nothing pursued us to the shore, for I'm uncertain we had the breath to turn and fight them. When we were close to the landing I had the war horn sounded, telling Signar we'd be on them in a moment, and in no mood to tarry.

The crew worked quickly, and in a few short moments all were aboard the longboats save Rhalgorn and two Vikonen, who had stayed behind to guard our rear. Signar sent every craft but one to the ships and we waited, weapons at hand, backs to the river. Soon, the the Stygiann and his party crashed out of the brush and stumbled to the boat, and we made our way quickly to the *Ahzir*.

Stygianns do not tire easily. They have extraordinary strength and endurance, and take much pride in doing the impossible. Rhalgorn, however, was beyond caring about such things for the moment. He lay back in the longboat, taking in great swallows of air. His eyes were closed, and his long red tongue hung limply from his muzzle.

"Your god-dream was not far from the truth," I told him. "We will turn on ourselves, and devour our own kind. It has much meaning to me now."

He nodded wearily, tasting the dryness in his throat. "God-dreams are always quite clear after they are over, Aldair. One would think the gods could simply come right out and say what's on their minds, instead of wrapping the facts in mystery. It would save mortal creatures a great deal of time and trouble."

"Then," I explained, "they would not be acting in the manner of gods."

He gave me a long, sober stare. "That would be perfectly all right with me."

Night was near bright as day aboard the *Ahzir*, *Aghiir*,

and *Shamma a'Lan*. Torches ringed the decks clear round, and Signar had ordered them lashed to long poles so they would extend several meters over the water. While I was certain no animals could reach us in the middle of the river, I thoroughly approved these precautions.

Naturally, the discovery of our two sentries and the encounter with the beasts spread quickly through our vessels. Sailors are a peculiar lot, and like to complain even when there is little to complain about. Now, they had a bone with some meat on it, and let us know their feelings.

This greatly angered Signar-Haldring, for though he is fair in all things, he is, in the end, a ship's captain. "I do not disagree with you in any way," I told him. "It is necessary to keep discipline aboard ship. Still, our crew is a good and loyal lot, and they know the cause they fight for. They faced something this morning that shook them to the core, and I don't think we can blame them for that."

Signar made a noise in his chest. "It's not *blame* I'm talkin' about," he said grimly. "Bein' scared's no sin, Aldair, and I'd not trust a fellow who claims he has no fear in the face of danger. This business is somethin' else again—they're scared of what they *can't* see, and figure that gives 'em the right to tell *me* how to run my ship. Would you have me give in to 'em on that?"

"No." I shook my head. "What I would do is tell them the truth, Signar. That there's indeed great danger on the shore. That if there's one sort of beast in Merrkia, there's bound to be others as well. They know we ran from something more than what we saw out there—tell 'em what it was. That the ancestors of the Stygianns took their companions. That they're out there now, and likely watching us close. Maybe some of *your* kind, too."

Signar's eyes told me he had certainly given some thought to this, and that he did not relish meeting prehistoric Vikonen any more than the rest of us.

"You may be right," he admitted finally. "What you're saying is real enemies is easier to face than some kinda spook or other in your head."

"Exactly."

"I'll do it, then, if it'll get everybody back to workin' straight. Though it seems to me what's real out there is a far sight *worse* than near anything they'd likely be imagining."

Thus, Signar-Haldring followed my suggestions regarding the crew. I think this was the proper thing to do, and I believe Signar agreed, for the most part. Neither of us realized we had not heard the last of this matter.

In the morning, we continued upriver. This was not to the crew's liking, for they imagined we would turn about after our venture ashore and head for the open sea. Signar made it clear he was tired of hearing where our ships should or shouldn't go, and that if anyone cared to discuss the subject further they had best bring a good sharp weapon to do the talking. No one took him up on this, and it was some time before we heard any more suggestions from the deck. Also, I think the crew was somewhat relieved to learn I intended to keep to the river, and not make camp ashore. Even the most skeptical among them felt that an animal would have to do quite a bit of swimming before it reached us.

Signar, Thareesh, Rhalgorn and Corysia all agreed with my decision. We were here, and safe enough while we kept to the river—if nothing else, we might learn how far the great city extended, and what else lay beyond. This last, I felt, was reason enough for going on. For though we had learned a great deal on the shores of Merrkia, we had done little to further our quest. We had solved the riddle of Hell-Dream, and the fate of Sergrid's people—but the answer told us little we needed to know. We had learned that beasts still abounded in the land—but we knew we were Man's creations, and how we'd started. We were still no closer to learning what we *needed* to learn—the knowledge that would help us break the chains of a history Man had forced upon us. Until such knowledge was ours, we would still belong to him.

I could not say what we would find up the broad river. Or whether we would find anything at all. That is the thing about a'venturing; it is very much like a soldier's game of dice. Until all your coppers are gone, there is ever a chance on the very next toss.

Twelve

Even Corysia admitted the flying device might serve us well on the venture upriver. This is not to say she encouraged the matter, but neither did she pout, wail, or make separate sleeping arrangements. Thareesh and I had given a great deal of thought to the major shortcoming of flying: namely, coming down again somewhat faster than a stone. A simple fabric valve had been installed in the rigging to enable us to release air at a reasonable speed; a decided advantage over slashing the bag to ribbons. In addition, using the device on the river was not nearly as hazardous as floating above the sea. It would not be necessary to sail far above the ship, as we could see all we needed to see from twice the height of the mast. Thus, we would avoid the problem of drag from high winds, which had brought us to disaster before. Neither of us relished the thought of losing our rope, and coming down in the wilds of Merrkia.

As my father used to say, he who thinks there are no surprises left in the world has never caught his foot in a hare trap. This bit of wisdom was brought home to me when Rhalgorn announced that he, too, would be accompanying us into the air.

"*You?*" I said. "Can it be I have lost an eye as well as an ear? Is this truly Rhalgorn, Lord of the Lauvectii, Thareesh?"

"Even if it is, which I doubt," Thareesh said soberly, "I would not think it wise to let him aboard. We know nothing of the effects of rabbit breath at high altitudes."

"This is true. It is something to consider."

"Or suppose he gets hungry, and eats the rigging?"

"There is that."

"It does not appear to be a sound idea."

"No, I am afraid Stygianns are not cut out for floating."

63

Rhalgorn waited patiently until we were finished. "I hope you enjoyed talking to one another," he said stiffly, "for I assure you I was not listening. Floating above the ground is most unseemly, and I have nothing but scorn for such business. However, as I have the only pair of eyes aboard which can see beyond the railing of the ship, I suppose I must put them to use."

With that, he turned and stalked off toward the bow of the *Ahzir*. It was early yet, and he had not had time to tell the Vikonen how to guide the ship properly, or why the sails should be set in one direction and not the other.

Since we did not deem it wise to crowd three aboard the small basket, I stayed below that afternoon while Thareesh took Rhalgorn aloft. All went well, and I was greatly pleased. It was a calm, nearly windless day, and the device floated straight above the mast. The controls worked beautifully, and Thareesh brought the thing down without incident at sundown.

"See," I told Corysia, "there is nothing to worry about. I expect you will be asking to go yourself quite soon."

Corysia gave me a baleful stare. "I will, Aldair. As soon as the clouds rain ale and barley beer."

Thareesh hopped down from the basket before it hit the deck, blood in his cold agate eyes. "*Now* the Stygiann knows all about floating devices, as well as ships," he fumed. "He is all yours, Aldair. I would as soon be skinned alive as go through *that* again!" With a last murderous glance at Rhalgorn, he stalked below making a great deal of noise—no easy feat for a Niciean.

Corysia and Signar could not stop laughing. Rhalgorn, looking pleased with himself, announced that he would prefer to be addressed as far-seer *and* master-flyer in the future.

At dawn on our second day upriver, I went aloft with Rhalgorn. The city of Man was still very much with us. Indeed, it seemed to have no ending. Pale fingers of stone stretched to the far horizon on either side, and even Rhalgorn far-seer found not a single patch of forest without some structure poking through its branches.

"Aldair, it cannot go on forever," he declared.

"I shouldn't think so. But it shows no sign of stopping."

"It will, though."

"Why do you say that?"

"Because it makes no sense to build so many things of stone."

"According to the Stygianns, it makes no sense to build *any* sort of structure."

"That's true," he agreed. "But even someone who did build them would not build as many as this. Thus, we will soon see an end to them."

This may explain why Thareesh did not fully enjoy his day aloft. There is only one form of logic to a Stygiann, and that is his own. He cannot understand why folk of other races refuse to act in a reasonable manner.

At noon, the sun broke through the clouds and the world below took on a brighter hue. The dark and somber forest turned green as new grass, and the ruins of Man sparkled like chips of marble. We pulled our lunch up on a rope from the *Ahzir,* and for some reason, Rhalgorn took great delight in this.

There was still very little to see of any interest. We knew there were creatures down there, but they were either well away from the river, or too well hidden for even Rhalgorn's uncanny sight. Occasionally, he would report a bug on a leaf, or a pebble at the bottom of the river, but I paid no attention to this. He felt obligated to see something after his fine speech the day before.

"It seems to me there should be *some* animals about," I said. "One or two, at least."

He peered at me over his muzzle. "So it would seem. But there are not."

"Why do you think we haven't spotted any?"

"Because there are none to see, Aldair. If there were, I would see them."

"I'm sure this is so."

"Do you doubt it?"

"Of course not. You are the far-seer. You told me so yourself."

"This is true. And master-flyer, as well, remember."

"I would not mention that last title around Thareesh, if I were you."

Rhalgorn made a face. "Niceans are most unreasonable creatures. Though I must add that I admire and respect

Thareesh—he is a good climber and a fair fighter for his size."

"It is nice of you to say so," I told him, getting a bit weary of this. "I suppose you have forgotten that the *unreasonable* Nicieans created a great culture below the Southern Sea. Stygianns, as I recall, are *still* living in the woods."

Rhalgorn looked puzzled. "Of course I have not forgotten, Aldair. I know the Nicieans founded an empire. So did the Rhemians. Both, if I am not mistaken, have come to a bad end. While as you say, the Stygiann people are *still* living in the forest of the Lauvectii."

It did not seem proper to let him get away with such a statement. What he said was true, but Stygianns tend to leave a great deal out of their stories. "Look," I began, "what you have failed to mention, Rhalgorn—"

He didn't hear me. At that moment, half a loaf of bread fell from his open jaws. He stared, wide-eyed, pointing a shaky finger at the river below. "The gods help us, Aldair! You wanted animals and there they are—every bedamned animal in the world, as far as I can tell!"

I near choked on a jug of ale. There they were indeed, just past the *Ahzir* beyond a narrow bend in the river. The banks were black with their hideous forms, and hundreds more swarmed out of the dark forest as we watched.

I sounded the warhorn to alert the vessels below. But it was already far too late for that...

Thirteen

It is a terrible thing to stand idle while good companions die. Surely, a warrior can suffer no greater shame than this. We could see everything—and do nothing. I longed for a bow and a quiver of arrows. They would have made little difference in the end, but at least I could have played some small part in the horror below. I have tried to set down events as I saw them from above the *Ahzir*, and if I have not conveyed the true agony and terror of those who lived that moment, it is because I was not there beside them, and will not put words to their suffering. Other than that, this is an accurate accounting, for I could see exactly what happened to each of our vessels. This was a knowledge tragically denied my captains, for they saw only a small part of the picture, and could not react quickly enough to avert disaster.

Plainly, the creatures had watched us and studied our vessels well, for they attacked with grim purpose and skill. The *Ahzir* led the way upriver, with the *Aghiir* and *Shamma a'Lan* close behind. Too close, as it happened—for their positions left little room for quick maneuvers.

Perhaps my warhorn gave Signar the precious seconds he needed; a moment more and the *Ahzir* would have sailed helplessly into the narrows. He turned the vessel hard to starboard, bringing it about so swiftly we nearly fell from our perch above. Bhaldrig, aboard the *Aghiir*, had little time to wonder with Signar was about. Clearly, he could not see what was waiting for him, as he sailed past the *Ahzir*, narrowly missing her stern, and made for the bend ahead. Now, even if there had been time for it, there was no room to turn about.

By this time, Captain Sheeshaan knew something was amiss. The *Aghiir* had nearly disappeared round the curve of the

river. The *Ahzir al'Rhaz* was full about, making way downriver. Signar had wisely put the crew to oars, wasting no time
on the sails. He signaled frantically to the *Shamma* to turn
about, but Sheeshaan could do nothing in the time he had,
for he had cut his speed too quickly and was drifting in the
water. It was a fatal mistake, and perhaps it could have been
avoided—but that's of little matter now.

I knew the *Aghiir* was gone, for she was caught in the
narrows, dead in the water. Great oaks grew over the river
there, and the beasts were dropping to her decks from above.
The vessel was near black with their bodies, and I could
scarcely see a warrior still standing.

By now, the shores on either side of the river were alive
with terrible creatures of every description, howling and roar-
ing for blood. This was an awesome sight, but I did not see
how they could endanger the *Ahzir* or *Shamma*. They had
taken the *Aghiir*, but not from deep water—and for all the
din they made none had strayed from the shore to reach us.
Signar was making for *Shamma* to get a line about her and
help Sheeshaan put good water under his hull. It was a tense
moment, and no time to dally about, but *Shamma* would
soon be out of danger. I am certain both Sheeshaan and
Signar believed this, too. . . .

When it happened, it happened quickly.

Signar was only moments from getting a line away. Sheeshaan had oars to water and was making way to meet him.
Then, of a sudden, from every point along the shore hundreds of crude wooden rafts splashed into the river, one
behind the other, until they jammed the shallows and spread
into the current beyond. A great and terrible cry rang from
the throats of the beasts—as one, they surged from the banks,
bounding from one raft to the other. In seconds, they were
clawing up the sides of *Shamma* and swarming onto her
decks.

I stared at the scene below, dumb with horror, and as
helpless to stop the carnage as Sheeshaan's desperate crew.
The beasts were terrible to behold, dark hordes of fur, fang
and claw. There were gaunt and rangy creatures with blood-
red eyes and snapping jaws, Rhalgorn's ancient kin. . . . great
burly animals bigger than Vikonen, and sleek as satin killers
that screamed like a tortured female.

There were scenes that day that will ever be etched in

my mind—companions raked in half by the path of a single paw, warriors crushed to the deck before they could strike a blow. More than once, I saw some fellow screaming in the grasp of a beast while it chewed a limb away. Often, an animal would stop to tear and eat its kill, and would angrily fend off several others to keep his prize.

The things could be stopped, but they did not die easily. They would fight on, maddened to greater fury, with half a dozen arrows in their hides. A sharp lance or war-axe was fairly effective, but swords did little good at all. These creatures were much too fast for the swing of a heavy blade. Our crewmen were seasoned fighters all, but they were no match for such a foe. Many dropped their weapons and leaped from the sides of the ship, and I cannot fault them for that. Sheeshaan and a small band held out for a moment, their backs to the bow, but they were soon overwhelmed and we saw them no more.

Signar knew in an instant there was little he could do for *Shamma*. Those who could reach the *Ahzir* were hauled quickly aboard, but he dared not waste a moment for those who could not. In this he was right, for though it pains a warrior to let companions die, it is folly to doom those still alive.

The Vikonen was out of peril for the moment; he had brought his sails to bear again and had every oar churning foam. Once out of the shallows, the rafts were next to useless, for they dispersed too quickly, and the animals could no longer bound from one to another. Some, maddened to see us beyond their reach, leaped without thinking into the river and paddled clumsily toward us. These were dispatched with grim determination by our bowmen, and each time a beast sank beneath the water, the crew lent a blood-yell to the action. It was little retribution for what we had suffered, but it was something.

Moments later, these cheers turned to groans of despair. I looked downriver and my heart sank. The beasts were not through with us yet. *Shamma* and *Aghiir* had been only the beginning, for the way ahead was now thick with rafts and howling creatures. Deep water would not save the *Ahzir* now—though many of the rafts would be swept away, they would take us by sheer numbers. If only a handful got aboard. . . .

Signar bellowed orders and the *Ahzir* surged forward. Our
rope went suddenly taut and jerked us hard against the side
of the basket. Rhalgorn looked startled. "Signar's getting all
the speed he can," I shouted. "The faster he goes, the more
we'll drag behind!"

"Then they had better pull us down," said Rhalgorn. "We
are getting lower by the minute."

I stared at him. For a master-flyer, he had learned precious
little. "There is too much pressure on the rope. They can*not*
pull us down. Even if—" I stopped, and a cold chill marched
up my back. "Rhalgorn—it is worse than that. *We* are drag-
ging *them* back, too!"

The Stygiann looked puzzled, then his eyes grew wide
with understanding.

"You see it, then. We are acting as a great anchor, slowing
them down." I glanced quickly over the side. There was less
than two-hundred meters between the *Ahzir* and the waiting
hordes.

"Signar could make it," Rhalgorn said bluntly. "But not
with us behind."

"No."

"Then they must cut the rope, Aldair. There is nothing else
for it."

I shook my head. "They won't. They will try to make it
without losing us. We must do it for them, Rhalgorn. And
we must do it now."

Rhalgorn said nothing. There was no real need for words.
His hand went to his belt and brought out a blade. He looked
at it a moment, then looked at me. Suddenly, a foolish grin
creased his muzzle.

"I see nothing amusing in this," I told him. "Do it, or I
will!"

"I think you will not," he said calmly. "I am not quite
ready to bathe in the river, Aldair, or fight my ancestors.
Here, hold still, now!" Before I could get a word out, he
whipped a length of cord from his waist, grabbed my hands
firmly, and bound them together. I thought for certain he'd
lost his mind. Just as quickly, he picked me up, thrust my
arms about his neck, and bounded out of the basket. Too
late, I realized what he was about.

"Rhalgorn, it'll never work!" I shouted in his ear.

"Probably not. Now close your snout and hang on. We do not have time to discuss the matter."

The moment he grabbed the rope, I knew we were done for. Our weight immediately dipped the floater at an alarming angle. A few meters later it trailed near straight behind us—and we were still not halfway to the *Ahzir.*

Rhalgorn's breath came in short, tortured gasps; the stubbornly forced one hand over the other, but he could not keep this up for long with my weight and his to carry. The floater was dropping fast. When it hit the water, so would we. And that would be that.

Still, Rhalgorn hung on. The stern of the *Ahzir* was only three meters away. Then two. Cold spray from her wake came up to meet us. We could make it! One moment more—

Rhalgorn uttered a terrible Stygiann curse and the rope slipped out of his hands. . . .

Fourteen

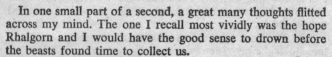

In one small part of a second, a great many thoughts flitted across my mind. The one I recall most vividly was the hope Rhalgorn and I would have the good sense to drown before the beasts found time to collect us.

I kept waiting for the water.

It seemed a long time coming.

Not that there was any great hurry. . . .

Suddenly, something thick and furry tightened across my back. Creator's Eyes, I thought, some terrible creature has snatched us from the air! Then I remembered that the beasts of Merrkia do not smell of salt and barley beer. Signar-Haldring staggered under his load, tumbled roughly to the deck, and buried us under his weight. For a brief moment, I found great joy in being stepped on by a Vikonen.

A crewman slashed leather from my wrists and pressed a blade in my hands. Another swung his great axe and loosed the rope from our stern. The *Ahzir* shuddered, and fair leapt across the water, free of her burden at last.

Racing to the bow to join the others, I spotted Corysia in the crowd—but there was no time for greetings. The way ahead was thick with beasts. As we watched, hundreds more took to the water, bounding across their rafts to meet us. There was wind in our sails and the crew plied oars for all they were worth. We sliced the dark waters at a fair pace, but we could not gain the speed one gets on the open sea. If we failed to break that tangle of logs and keep going. . . . If they held us for only a moment. . . .

Thirty meters. Then twenty. Warriors lined the rails, and every weapon aboard was brought to bear against the beasts. They were good targets, and we tumbled them to the river by the dozens. Still they kept coming.

Ten meters. Five. Suddenly, we were in the midst of them,

and above the terrible din of the creatures came the sharp crack of timber in our bow. For a moment, I was certain we'd gone dead in the water. Then, from the cheers behind me I knew we were still under way. Open jaws and blood-red eyes clambered up the rail, then fell back howling. Somewhere, a warrior screamed. A dark gray shape crouched on the bow and I loosed an arrow in its chest. The beast snarled, snapped at the missile with its teeth, and kept coming. One arrow, then another hummed past my shoulder and the thing dropped at my feet, teeth still snapping.

A great bellow shook the decks and I jerked around. Above me, on the bridge, the ancestor of all Vikonen towered over Signar, clawing the air with enormous paws. It had made its way amidships from the stern, leaving a bloody path behind —now, it had a foe it truly relished. Signar's weapon flashed. A furry arm swept it aside and sent it clattering across the deck. Signar fell back. A black-furred warrior, one of Raadnir's own, stepped boldly in the creature's way and buried a war-axe clear to the hilt in its belly. The beast roared, lashing out blindly in its pain. The Vikonen calmly stepped under those awesome limbs and wrapped his arms tightly about the thing's chest. Bracing his boots, he strained against the creature with all the strength he could bring to bear. The beast swayed, tumbled to the deck below. The rail splintered, gave way, and both beast and warrior vanished beneath the water.

Quite suddenly, it was over. . . .

The beasts fell back behind us, and our oars once more churned water. There was no great call for speed, now, but the crew seemed not to notice, and put their backs to the task.

One final tale must be recorded here to properly close the chronicle of Hell-Dream. It is no more pleasant than what has gone before, but without it, the story is not complete. Minutes after we left the beasts in our wake, Rhalgorn called me quietly to the rail. After Signar and the Nicean joined us, he pointed to the shore. "No doubt you thought there were few surprises left in the land of Merrkia," he said darkly. "If you will take a look over there you will find another. I do not think you'll need the eyes of a Stygiann to see all you care to see."

I looked, and for a moment it seemed that nothing was there, for they blended so well with the grays and greens of

the forest. Then, as if a veil had been lifted from my eyes,
I saw them, still and silent as shadows. The beasts themselves
were terrible to behold, but their masters were nightmares
come to life. This, of course, is what they had to be, for
though we'd given no thought to such things in the heat of
battle, animals do not bind logs and vines together for rafts.
And even the most cunning among them could not have devised the plan that brought our vessels to ruin.

It is difficult to describe these things, for a picture of one
tells little about another. They were neither Man nor animal,
but something in between. There were creatures with hooves
and paws and limbs such as ours. Things with snouts or
muzzles or tiny slits beneath their eyes. . . . Things furred
or scaled or mottled with hair and raw pink skin. . . . For
all they had done against us, it was hard to view them without
pity or sorrow. They could be neither more nor less than
what they were, for their ancestors had been made-things,
like our own, and they had not been asked what they would
like to be.

Here, I thought, was the most shameful work of Man. If
we were his creatures, at least we had not changed greatly
from our beginnings. He had not turned us into monsters,
or pressed the abomination of his own seed upon us.

The shore was empty. Both beast and master had slipped
back to the shadows of their terrible world. On every side,
there was only the green of the forest, and the pale white
fingers of ancient places.

"Leavings," Thareesh said quietly. "That's what they are,
Aldair. The scraps of Man's damnable tampering."

"I am afraid you are right," I said.

"We are all here, then—the beasts, the leavings, and the
final creation. All we need is Man to complete the picture."

"I'm *damned* if we do," growled Signar.

Later that evening we smelled the good salt air of the sea,
and we did not tarry till the dark coast of Merrkia was well
behind us. Of the thirty crewmen aboard the *Aghiir* all were
lost to the beasts. Twenty-six perished aboard *Shamma a'Lan*;
only nine from that vessel made it safely to the *Ahzir*. During
our last encounter with the animals, eight crewmen were

killed, and three more would die of their wounds before the day was out.

It was not a battle such as any we had fought before. Death came quickly, and there was little time for honor, bravery, or noble deeds. Though few care to admit it, there is very little glory in the soldiering trade—regardless of the foe you're facing. For the most part, it is a fine opportunity to die painfully, with no particular notice.

Fifteen

———◆——◆——◆———

There is little need to recount those first few days at sea. Nothing of great interest occurred, and this pleased us all. We sailed south, keeping the shores of Merrkia in sight to starboard. Signar complained that our encounter with the rafts had weakened our bow somewhat, cracking a few timbers and causing leakage down below. However, when I asked if he wished to find harbor and attend to these matters, he bluntly informed me that we were damaged, not sinking, and that he would swim ahead and tow the *Ahzir* in his teeth before he would make port in that land again.

Since our venture upriver, Signar had not been the most pleasant of companions. As captain of our fleet, he blamed himself in a hundred different ways for that disaster. Of course, it had been my decision to make the journey, but this mattered little to the Vikonen.

The tragedy of Hell-Dream was in all our minds, but we seldom spoke of it. Perhaps we feared our words might bring some horror of that day to life again. . . . Or hoped our silence would turn back the hours, and erase those moments from the past.

Clearly, I was not entirely right in this, for I learned that certain members of our crew were talking of little else. Signar did his best to put a stop to the business, but even his strong hand was to no avail. Finally, a fight broke out below decks, and one fellow did a little carving on another. At this point, I stepped into the matter and had the two brought before me. I did not ordinarily interfere in such things, but I had a special interest in this particular case—the pair involved were the only other members of my race aboard the *Ahzir*, save Corysia.

The first, Stumbaucius, was a former legionnaire. Our paths had crossed briefly on a day long past, when I stole Corysia from her Rhemian guards. She spotted him again among the hungry throng fleeing the dying Empire. We took him aboard, and he turned into a fair seaman. He was a stout, grizzled campaigner, and knew how to take an order and carry it out without question.

This Barthius, now, was of another stripe altogether. He had served aboard one of those vessels the Rhemians term ships o'war, and the Niceans and Vikonen call ungainly washtubs. After our sentries were slain and we took to the river, it was Barthius who started the crew complaining.

Of the two, I greatly favored the soldier Stumbaucius. He seemed a simple, honest fellow, especially next to the other. Barthius had the short snout and square head of the Belaturri. Ragged 'ears hung nearly to his jowls and his body was covered with black and auburn hair. The Belaturri have ever been millers by trade, and a surly lot at best. Clearly, good sea air did little to improve their tempers.

When I asked who'd started the fight, it was Barthius who blurted out an answer. "That one," he said angrily, "it was him started the thing an' me doing nothin' but going about my business! He—"

I cut him off quickly. "Is this true, Stumbaucius?"

"Yes, sir. It is." The soldier looked straight at me, making no attempt to turn away.

"There's no good reason to take a blade to *anyone* aboard this vessel," I told him. "No doubt, though, you've one to tell me."

"Yes, sir, I do."

"And what might it be?"

"I—didn't like what he was saying."

"You cut him because you didn't care for his words."

"Yes, sir."

"I'd hear what they were, then."

Barthius opened his mouth to protest, but he needn't have bothered. Stumbaucius bit his jowls and looked to the deck. "Your pardon, sir. I'd rather not say."

"*Damn* you!" I shouted, bringing a fist down hard on the table, startling them both. "I care not a whit what you'd *rather* or rather *not*, fellow! Out with it, now!"

Stumbaucius swallowed hard. He was stuck with a dilemma he didn't care for. On the one hand, it almost pained him to disobey an order. On the other—and just as strong—was the unwritten soldier's code, which held him from speaking against a comrade, no matter what the circumstances. I had no desire to punish him, for I was certain Barthius had gotten exactly what he deserved. Still, his silence left me little choice.

"Thirty days double watch," I told him, "and half rations as well. Perhaps you'll think twice about pulling your blade on another."

Stumbaucius blinked not an eye at the sentence, but a sly grin started at the curve of Barthius' mouth. He caught himself quickly, but I saw him plain enough.

"Does this seem fair to you?" I asked him. "It was you who took the cut."

"Sir, it's right and just as I see it," he said soberly.

"Good. For you'll be serving with him, my friend."

Barthius' jaw fell. "That's not—"

"*Fair*, Barthius? Creator's Eyes but you're a poor excuse for a sailor, and I'm ashamed to call you one of my own!" The more I saw of this fellow, the less I liked him. "—And I'll tell you one thing more, and trust you don't forget it. If I'd tolerate the lash aboard the *Ahzir*, you'd be the first to feel it!"

"Sir, I—" Barthius opened his mouth and searched for words. "Sir, I didn't do nothing—nothing at all!"

"You did a great deal more than Stumbaucius here. At least h cuts with an honest blade, while you've no more than a mouth. I don't *need* to hear what he has to say about you, for I can guess it well enough. Everyone aboard has heard your words but me. Now—" I stood, and walked around the table to face him. "Suppose we get to the bottom of this, Barthius."

Our talk was not going the way Barthius had in mind. "There's—nothing, sir."

"There'd better be," I warned him. "If there's not, I'll double the punishment you've got, and you can spend the rest of the voyage counting seagulls. Do you hear me well?"

"Yes, sir. I—do." He knew for certain I'd do just as I promised.

"It's the crew, sir."

"The crew?"

"Yes, sir. They feel—I mean—"

"They, Barthius? You speak for the crew, do you?"

"No indeed, sir. It's just that some of them feel—"

"No," I stopped him. "I do not care to hear what *you* think someone else may feel. I am interested in what you think, yourself."

"Sir—"

"Do not push me, Barthius."

He let out a deep sigh, deciding he had indeed tested me as far as he dared. "All right, Master Aldair," he said wearily, "I'll tell you, then, even if it costs me my hide, for it's something you ought to hear, an' I'm not the only one sayin' it, for certain!"

"Barthius—"

"Yes, sir. Well—sir, I grant you we all came aboard knowing the cause we're fighting for and that there'd be dangers and all, but—" He hesitated, then blurted it out. "Sir, we're none of us coming back from all this 'less you get us away from this terrible land and back where we belong! There aren't *many* left of us *now*—and we'll all be dead soon enough if you don't stop chasin' after—after nothing at all! You just—" He stopped, shaking in his boots now, suddenly aware he'd gone a great deal further than he'd intended.

I leaned back against the table and looked at him. "Back where, Barthius? East, to Rhemia and a world that's crumbling to ruin as we speak? North, to Raadnir and beyond, and a winter sea that'd freeze the snout from your face? I know you'd not turn west to the land of Merrkia. *South* is where we're headed, and if I decide to go straight up or straight *down* from there, you'll not open your mouth against it." I took a step forward and laid a finger against his chest. "Listen, and listen well, Barthius—if you speak another foul word to this crew I'll put you ashore to starboard and let you try your mouth with *those* creatures! Now—get out of my sight the both of you, and be smart about it!"

Thus, I believed this encounter would bring an end to the matter, and dismissed it from my mind. Someday perhaps I will learn that the wisdom of my fathers is good for a great deal more than putting young children to sleep. If I recall the saying correctly, it states there are two kinds of fools in the world—one imagines a turnip is smiling, the other imagines it isn't. Like all good sayings, it makes little sense until it is far too late to be of value.

Sixteen

—————◄►———◄■►———◄►—————

Some ten days after we left the mouth of the river, the land to starboard changed greatly. There were still dark oaks to see, but now their branches were heavy with thick beards of moss. Tall pines and firs appeared, and where a river met the sea there was a peculiar kind of tree that stalked out into the water on its roots. A few days later, sandy beaches came down to touch the foam, and the land was filled with birds of every size and color. Once, we glimpsed a flock of dazzling pink creatures with graceful necks and long spindly legs. When they saw us, and took to the air, their numbers near blotted out the sun.

The sea and the weather favored us as well; the air was clear and warm and the water a vibrant blue. It was a pleasant scene to follow, but like all things, it had both a beginning and an end. One fine dawning, the land of Merrkia gave way abruptly to the open sea.

Before, it had been easy enough to put off decisions about the future. If we did not know what was ahead, we knew all too well what lay behind. We could follow the curve of the land, or continue southward to—what? Was there another land below, or nothing at all? In my encounter with Barthius, I had acted the bold leader, convinced of my destiny. In my own mind, I was less certain where we were, and where we were going. In the meantime, we had a pressing need to find safe harbor. We were low on water and provisions, and Signar-Haldring vowed he woud not continue on *any* course without a look at our bow. Thus, it seemed we had no choice in the matter. It was the shore of Merrkia or none at all— and I was not at all sure we could find a crewman willing to set his boots on that soil again.

In the end, we made no decision at all, but put it off for the moment. To the south of the mainland, the sea was dotted with small islands or keys, and though none seemed promising from afar, we convinced ourselves they were worth looking over. In spite of the manner in which many fine tales are told, this is the way most bold ventures come about.

Fortune set her eyes upon us that day, for before the sun dropped into the sea we found an isle that suited our needs. It was large enough to fill our wants, and small enough to assure us it harbored no enemies. Early the next morning, Rhalgorn and Thareesh led four Niciean warriors ashore to look the place over. This party was chosen because each of its members could run extremely fast. Less than an hour later, they were back on the white beach jumping about and waving us to shore. . . .

There was a spring on the isle, and while the water was slightly bitter, we gladly filled our casks to the brim. Provisions were not in great abundance, and consisted mostly of sour fruits and wild vegetables such as leeks and onions. Nevertheless, we stripped the place bare of everything it offered, and dried great quantities of fish and other sea creatures in the sun. The smell of this process offended Rhalgorn no end, and he could not imagine why the place did not have fine plump hares to eat.

"There are hares aplenty on the shores of Merrkia," I pointed out. "It is only a few leagues back, and I'm sure Sigmar would loan you a longboat."

The Stygiann gave me a sober stare. "If he thought I'd go, he would row me there himself."

Since I began my misadventures, a number of things have happened which defy explanation. I have spoken before of those beings who share my cause, and set me on this path in some mysterious manner: Lord Tharrin, Aghiir of Niciea, who first revealed to me the true age of ancient places; Nhidaaj, the Cygnian, who was a slave and not a slave at all. And finally, that strange and awesome seer with eyes like almonds set on end, who is master of them all.

Dreams of places I have never been have graced my sleep. Sometimes, I feel my seer has sent these sights to grant me understanding. At others, I feel the things I see are the result of too much barley beer before bedtime.

Still, it is hard to imagine I have unerringly stumbled into trouble on my own, over and over again. Albion, the towers of Indrae, the Great Wastes above the land of the Avakhar. Perhaps it's true that I am a link in some great and purposeful chain of events—some mission that will one day unlock the secrets of Man. I like to think so, and at times I am almost able to believe this. At others, I remember that every radish in the garden doubtless sees himself as the only one in his row the sun has truly blessed.

Two days after we landed on the isle, something happened which led me to believe I might—just possibly—be a radish of some note after all. Corysia and I were enjoying the sun, and one another, when Thareesh came bounding down the beach, his long green tail whipping like a pennant behind him. I sat up and took note of this, for Niceans are not overly excitable creatures. When he was nearly upon us, I saw that he carried some long flat object in his arms.

"Aldair," he said, catching his breath, "I have been looking all over for you. This is a thing you must see!"

I glanced at the item in his hands, which seemed no more than a flat and crusted scrap of wood. I knew there were minor ruins on the isle, but I had truly had by fill of such places for the moment.

"What is it," I asked him, "another artifact?"

"No," he said evenly, for he could see I was less than enthusiastic. "It is not just *any* artifact, Aldair." I said no more, but let him lead us out of the sun and into the shade off the beach. He dropped to the ground and crossed his legs, placing the object on the sand before us.

"At first," he said, "I thought it nothing more than it appears to be—some Man-thing that has little meaning. Then, I turned it on its edge and noticed this. You see? It is glass, Aldair, or the substance much like it we found in such profusion in Merrkia."

We bent to look at the thing, and Corysia laid a finger along its edge. "It is not one piece of glass-stuff, but two. See there, Thareesh. They have been fused together."

"Burned, probably," I suggested.

"Exactly," beamed the Nicean. Now—" He turned the object flat again. "Note that it is covered in wood dust and dirt, pressed hard as stone by the ages. Yet, it comes off easily enough with a little scraping." Putting his blade to work, he began chipping pieces of debris into his lap. He was right—the stuff came off with little effort. Something lay beneath all this, but I could not tell what it might be, for Thareesh held it close to his chest, out of my sight.

"I know what's there," he said, agate eyes shining, "for I chipped a small piece away at the site. I did no more, Aldair, because I wanted you to be present when it was finally uncovered. Corysia—would you be kind enough to bring me a jug of water?" She stood and ran back to the beach where we'd left our provisions.

"Thareesh," I said, "this is no time to stop for a drink. I would like to see what you have there."

"Patience, Aldair." He held a single finger before my face. "You have lived among Niceans long enough to learn the value of waiting."

"I have lived among the Venicii, too," I told him, "and I assure you patience is not one of our better qualities. Thareesh—"

"Ah, there now." He took the jug from Corysia and poured a good deal of water over the edge of his cloak. Then, he proceeded to soak the artifact thoroughly. When he was finished, he held it up and stared. "By the Creator, it is even more than I imagined! Here, Aldair—I give you the world, or a good part of it, I'll wager."

I grabbed the thing from him and turned it about. Corysia gasped, and my heart near came to a stop, for Thareesh was as good as his word. There before me was a Man-chart, a map of his world with every nation and city clearly marked upon it! With a hand I could not keep from trembling, I found the places I knew—though the names, of course, were not the same: Gaullia, Albion Isle, the boot of Rhemia, and below it, the immense continent of Kanyarsha that looks all the world like a great skull. Across the Misty Sea was the land I guessed was Sergrid Bad-Beard's, and below that, Merrkia—though it was spelled in a slightly different manner. Down the eastern coast I traced our route to land's end, and the keys where we rested now. I shook my head in wonder. Could the world truly be as vast as this? Why, we had scarcely seen a small part of it! There were great islands, whole continents—even an *ocean* we had never known!

Beneath us, I saw the western continent became smaller, almost pinched to nothing in the center. Then, it spread to form another land, far to the south. On the eastern bulge of that continent, a great river met the sea. It was so vast it seemed every drop of water in the land must eventually come to rest there. Touching the twisted lines with my finger, I could almost—almost—

—*Quite suddenly, I was simply no longer there. . . . Something picked me up and wrenched me out of myself, and for the terrible part of a second Corysia, Thareesh, and all about me disappeared. I was nowhere. I could see nothing. Yet I knew it was a place I had been before, and that if I stayed there an instant longer—Corysia! Corysia—!*

"Aldair—are you all right!"

I opened my eyes. "I—called you. You weren't there. . . ."

"Yes," she said gently, "I am here, Aldair."

Thareesh handed me the jug of water, concern in his black-agate eyes. I pushed the water aside and picked up the Man-chart. "There," I pointed, and my hand was shaking so badly I pressed it to the map to hold it still. "There is where we must go, Thareesh."

The Niciean looked puzzled. "There? Why, Aldair?"

"Why? Because—" I couldn't think. I shook my head, feeling weak and foolish. "I don't know, Thareesh. I don't know. . . ."

"It has a name," said Corysia, squinting at the chart. "It is called Amazon."

"Yes," I told her, "I know." And I did.

Seventeen

Only the Creator can know every path we follow, and how each tale must end. Yet, there are times when I believe we can glimpse some small part of this great picture ourselves. And when I doubt that there is purpose and direction in my life, I need only recall the most unlikely turns of fate that brought me to this moment.

If we had not discovered the land of Raadnir. . . .

If Sergrid Bad-Beard had not used ancient charts as bait to lose a brother and gain a maiden. . . .

If we had not been attacked by the beasts of Merrkia and cracked our bow. . . .

If we had not picked one particular isle to repair our damage. . . .

If Thareesh had overlooked that impressive scrap that hid so much. . . .

If . . . if . . . if. . . . One can go on and on with this sort of thing until his head begins to swim.

Of course, it can be argued that such talk is no more than the pitiful dream of a beast who has been set on two legs and taught to mimic his makers. After the traitor Fabius Domitius plundered the secrets of Albion and held me in his keep, he did his best to convince me this was so. "Aldair," he said, "how can you *know* your fight to break the chains of history is not, after all, simply a part of the history they planned for us in the first place? Wouldn't it be the perfect joke of Man— *letting his creatures think they've broken free?*"

I will admit that in moments of dark despair, this thought has crossed my mind. There have been times when I would agree with Fabius' frightening logic: that if there is indeed a Creator, he is surely not ours; that if we wish to name a maker, we will have to call him Man.

This, I will not do.

Not long after we left our isle and sailed southwest through the great gulf below Merrkia, we came to another very much like the first. It was small, with sand as white as new-milled flour. Beyond it, just to the west, we could see the mainland, and knew by the charts of Man it was called Yucatan. Though what this meant, I cannot say.

Thareesh and Rhalgorn rowed ashore there, against my judgment, for I no longer trusted any piece of land broader than I could spit across. They were back quite soon, for Rhalgorn had scented wild creatures about, and seen their spoor. Thareesh reported he had glimpsed a peculiar ruin in the distance, and from his description it seemed much like the awesome pyramids I saw below Xandropolis, the night I met the seer with eyes like pumpkin seeds.

Certainly, after our experience in Hell-Dream, I think my fear of unknown lands was more than justified. To me, it seemed a sound idea to follow the coast which curved south and east to the great continent below. There were small islands hugging the shore along the way, and these, hopefully, would provide our needs. If they did not, we would risk a foray ashore. For awhile, we considered charting a course through the long chain of islands which lay south and east of the mainland of Merrkia. We had passed one of these to port, just after we made repairs on the *Ahzir*. Signar argued against this, and I agreed. Though these isles would provide us with a greater opportunity to replenish our supplies, they were large enough, for the most part, to harbor both beasts and half-beasts of every description.

"Besides," said the Vikonen, "you keep callin' this thing a *chart*, Aldair, and it ain't nothing of the sort. A chart shows depths and currents and the like—things a seaman can put to use. Now, this is a fine *map*, I'll grant you, but it falls way short of being a proper chart."

In addition, he said, sailing among islands could be a tricky business at best. Winds and currents are less predictable there than in the open sea—and we had already noted, at our isle off the place called Yucatan, that the beautifully colored growths just below the water were as sharp as any blade, and could easily rip the bottom out of a ship.

Thus, we kept to our southward course, always keeping

the land in sight to starboard. Strong offshore winds sent us swiftly along our way, and we found little use for our oars. The weeks passed quickly—cool, pleasant nights following balmy days, one upon the other. We passed the spot on our map where only a narrow strip of land connects the northern continent to the south. I felt a quick chill of wonder at this, knowing that only a few leagues away lay another great ocean, the largest in the world. It would take a bold seaman indeed, I decided, to brave such a sea!

To the east, then, and slightly north awhile, before we plunged southeastward down the long hump of the southern continent. Sometimes, we saw the treacherous fin of a shark following our wake. More than once, we caught flashes of silver in the distance as some graceful creature broke the water and mirrored the sun on his sides. There were fish that flew—or at least glided over the water a few meters. Rhalgorn did not believe this until Signar caught one and put it in his bed. The crew learned to capture these creatures with nets held over the sides—it was fine sport, and furnished us with many delicious dinners. The Stygiann, of course, would not touch them. He claimed that any creature who was unable to make up his mind whether to be a bird or a fish was not a seemly thing to eat.

We stopped at several small islands. For the most part, they were disappointing, having little food and no water. Finally, we risked a party ashore on the mainland, where a narrow stream met the sea. The crew did not loiter at this task, and in a matter of minutes we had fresh fruit and water aboard. Our bowmen shot several small deer, and even a few animals Rhalgorn said were hares, and therefore rightfully his. They did not resemble hares in any way whatever, but we were glad enough to let him have them. There is nothing like a hare—or even a quasi-hare—to improve a Stygiann's surly disposition.

Many things happen at sea which cannot be readily explained. Every sailor has a tale or two concerning strange sights and sounds from the deep. One can hear reports of monsters of every sort—great serpents with eyes like burning coals; terrible creatures with long, writhing arms that can pull a ship to the depths. There are even lovely maidens, it seems, who lure hapless mariners to their doom with a haunting song.

(Interestingly enough, these beings always seem to resemble the females of the particular sailor's race.)

While I do not put a great deal of stock in such stories, I will mention one peculiar sighting which is more than a sea-man's yarn, for I saw it myself. Indeed, it became such a common occurrence I doubt there was a soul aboard who did not witness it at one time or another. It began soon after we started down the eastern coast of the southern continent. We saw the things only at night, usually when the sea was un-usually calm. They would appear in the distance off our bow, and looked all the world like the heads of some creature bobbing in the water. Ordinarily, they came in groups of five or six, but several times a sailor reported there were too many around us to count. They never came close enough to let us see what they were, and as far as we could tell they meant us no harm. Without fail, these creatures would disappear be-neath the water when the *Ahzir* came too close to their position.

Corysia and I watched them from the bow one night when the moon spread silver on the water. I noted there seemed to be more of the creatures about than usual, and she agreed.

"Perhaps they are as fascinated by the moon as we are, Aldair."

"That's an interesting thought," I told her. "If there were reasoning creatures beneath the sea, what indeed would they think of the moon?"

"Why, the same as we, I imagine."

"Would they, though? The surface of the ocean must be the top of the world to those below. What a surprise to poke your head up through the ceiling, and find there's a great deal more beyond."

Corysia laughed lightly.

"What?"

"Nothing. I just had a mental picture of some creature suddenly—oh, look! There they are again!"

This time, they surfaced to port. Closer, it seemed, than ever before. Forty, maybe fifty of the creatures, drifting in the warm, moonlit waters.

"Aldair, sometimes they make me very—uncomfortable," Corysia whispered, locking her arm in mine.

"Uncomfortable?"

"Like they're—watching us."

"Why, they are, Corysia. Just as we're watching them."

"I *know* that," she said impatiently, "but that's not what I mean. I mean—*watching* us."

"Oh."

"You know exactly what I'm talking about."

"I guess I do," I admitted. "Maybe I'm just trying *not* to."

Corysia gave me a questioning look. "Not to what?"

"Think everything is watching me."

"Oh. I'm sorry, I guess I was—"

"No, not you, Corysia. Me. Us. Everyone aboard the *Ahzir*. And damn me, with good reason, too. Why shouldn't we think everything's watching us? So far, it—"

I stopped, seeing no clear reason to pursue the topic further. When everyone about you is thinking the same depressing thoughts, there is little comfort in bringing them to light. Seaman Barthius would have been proud of me—I was doing my part to lower morale.

"It's getting chilly up here," I told Corysia. "I think a cup of hot wine would serve us well." Corysia readily agreed, and we hurried below. Neither the moon nor the sea had change, but neither seemed as friendly as they had before.

Eighteen

For two more nights the sea creatures stayed with us. On the third, they were gone. We wondered at this, but not for long—an event of far greater interest had captured our attention. At dawn on the fourth day we woke to find the sea had changed its color overnight. It was no longer a deep, azure green, but a pale and sandy shade of yellow. This seemed quite peculiar to me, but not to Signar-Haldring. The broad grin across his muzzle said he had a ready answer to this happening, and would gladly give it if someone were to ask.

"All right, great mariner," I said finally, "it is clear you know something the rest of us do not. What's the matter with the ocean?"

Signar didn't answer, but dipped a jug with a long cord over the side, brought it back up, and handed it to me.

"What am I supposed to do with this?"

"Taste it."

I shook my head. "Thanks for your kindness, but I am not thirsty enough at the moment to drink sea water."

"Damn me, Aldair," he said irritably, "I ain't askin' you to drink it down like barley beer—just *taste* it!"

I looked at him, decided he had not lost his senses, and took a small sip from the jug. Then I took another. Suddenly, it occurred to me this was no ordinary sea water. It was nearly fresh, with only the slightest touch of salt. "All right," I said, "you have made your point. Now I am supposed to say: how can this be, Signar? One does not ordinarily find fresh water in the sea."

Signar grinned and pointed a big hand toward the far shore. "It can be, because we are there, Aldair."

"There where?"

"Where you wished to go. For only a river as mighty as the one on your map could thrust its waters far into the sea."

I stared. "The—*Amazon?*"

"Indeed it is." He shook his head in wonder. "I wouldn't believe it 'less I was standing here right on top of it, but that's what she is. There's no tellin' how many leagues it goes out past us, either. Might be a hundred or more."

It was a staggering thought, even though the map made it quite clear the great river drained near half a continent. Signar could not say when we'd reach the river's mouth, but guessed we'd see it by the end of the day, as we were already in its waters.

"I'll say this," I told him, "you have done a masterful bit of navigating, old friend. We've come a great many leagues through strange waters, and even with a good chart to go by—"

"*Map*, Aldair." He made a noise in his throat. "Like I said before, it ain't no chart. And though I thank you for your words, gettin' here isn't exactly what I'd call *navigating*— near anyone who can rig a sail shouldn't have no trouble following a coastline in the right direction. Why, I reckon even rabbit-breath could—" He stopped, looking appalled at his words. "Creator's Eyes, Aldair, the heat must be gettin' to me. Rhalgorn couldn't float a stick in a pond without sinkin' it sure!"

I laughed. "Apparently, great minds think much alike. It was only last night at supper that Rhalgorn stated Signar-Haldring could not find a tree in the woods without a good map."

"Chart," growled Signar, "an' he's wrong as he can be, 'cause I wouldn't be caught in no damp and moldy woods in the first place!"

Signar never asked just what I had in mind, now that we neared the great river. Neither did the others. If they questioned the wisdom of our course, they said nothing. Certainly, I could not have blamed them if they wondered what we might be doing at a place called Amazon, some thousand leagues from nowhere. In truth, I had no good answer to give them. For the beat of a heart on that isle at the end of Merrkia, I had *been* to that river, and *known* we would go there. Beyond that, there was nothing. And perhaps if my companions had seen the fear that touched me in that one small moment, they would have had a great deal more to say about our venture. . . .

Signar was wrong about the river. We did not reach its mouth that evening. Indeed, it was well past noon the next day before we discovered it truly had no single mouth at all, but a great many. The map had not made this overly clear, but we could see with our eyes that it was so.

"I don't suppose it matters which path we take," I told Signar. "They will all lead us inland, eventually."

"I reckon you're right," he muttered darkly, "so if it's all the same to you, let's find a good *wide* one." I could not argue with that. We had not been too successful sailing up rivers. I told him to find a way that suited him, and went below.

Now that we were sailing cautiously along the shore, the fine winds we'd enjoyed at sea left us abruptly, and the air became abominably hot and sticky. There was more to it than that, of course, for one could see by the map we were near the very center of the world, where the sun vents its greatest fury. Tracing a finger east, I could find the point parallel to our own off the coast of Kenyarsha, which the map calls Afrique. Though we'd had no charts to guide us when the *Ahzir al'Rhaz* rounded that continent, it was easy to remember how hot we'd been along those shores.

For awhile, I tried to close my eyes and doze, but the cabin was even more stifling than the decks above. Soon, I was floating in a pool of my own sweat—too miserable to get up or stay where I was. Finally, I dropped into a fitful sleep. The heat immediately obliged and sent me comforting dreams: terrible creatures fumbled outside the cabin, bumping against the door. They made an awful din, and I decided if they bumped any harder they'd come right through, and that would be that. Again. And again. Damn me, one more time and—

I sat up, suddenly awake. The whole vessel groaned and shuddered; something scraped loudly against her hull. The *Ahzir* gave a jerk, tilted dizzily to port, and tossed me to the floor. I was up and bounding for the deck before the noise came to an end.

"Signar!" I blinked against the sun. "What in all the hells was *that!*"

The Vikonen picked himself up and brushed off his jacket. "Wasn't nothin' more than a sandbar," he said stiffly. "You can figure on 'em with a river the size of that one at your back."

"Did we do any damage—Creator's Eyes, I thought we were going all the way down!"

"Well we ain't," he scowled. "Which isn't sayin' it couldn't have happened." I noted the ship had righted itself, and was bobbing about free and clear. "I wouldn't want to count on luckin' by too many of those," he added, "and it isn't gonna be that easy to get around 'em." He spit distastefully over the side. "The water here's 'bout as deep as a keg of ale after a two-day drunk!"

Rhalgorn trotted up from the stern, looking blandly about. "I don't think it's a very good idea to let the boat run over things, Signar."

Signar glared. "It's a *ship*, rabbit-breath. It ain't no boat. And I'll thank you to keep your navigatin' suggestions to yourself!" Rhalgorn shrugged and tried to look injured.

I turned to Signar. "Do you see a way upriver that suits our needs?"

"There's enough of 'em that'll do the job," he said, "but it's not all as easy as we figured. Close up like we are now you can see what's been happening. This Amazon of yours has got to be near as old as the world itself, Aldair. It's been dumping sand and dirt here forever an' I'd guess there's flats out there you could walk on."

"Places the *Ahzir* can't cross, you mean."

"Exactly. 'Less you want to chance leavin' the ship high and dry somewhere, we're going to have to take it real slow and easy."

"Then do what you have to," I told him. "I do not think I would be happy living on a sandbar."

It was a long and tedious afternoon. We placed extra lookouts in the rigging to search the way ahead, but soon found this did little good—the water was too sandy to tell depths from shallows. More than that, even the sun-loving Niceans who went aloft could take the heat for no more than a few minutes at a time. Eventually, we abandoned that business and sent a longboat ahead of the *Ahzir* to plumb the water with poles. It was slow, but certain, and as the crewmen got used to the task we began to move a little faster.

"I know you do not care for suggestions," said Rhalgorn, "even if they are good ones."

"I'm glad you understand that," said Signar.

Nevertheless, it appears to me we are encountering *more* of the dirt places on this course, rather than less, as we should be."

"*Sand*bars," snapped Signar. "Not dirt places!"

"Whatever. Still, this is true, is it not?"

Signar squinted over the brassy waters. "There's bars wherever you look. I don't see no more *here* than anyplace else."

"You may be right," yawned Rhalgorn.

"I am."

"It may be that it merely *seems* as if there are more because they move about so much."

Signar turned on him. "What are you talking about?"

"The sand places. As I said—"

"Sand*bars*. And they don't move around, Rhalgorn. They sit perfectly still."

"Oh," said the Stygiann. "I did not understand this. I am only a poor blind warrior making my way round the world." Signar muttered something under his breath.

"Rhalgorn, did you see something or didn't you?" I asked him.

"Clearly not, Aldair. I am merely a far-seer and master-flyer, not a great ship's captain."

"Rhalgorn—"

"However," he sniffed, "if you would care to look at something that is not to be seen, watch the sand places to port. While fat-fur was explaining the stillness of such things, two of them disappeared, and six others rose above the water."

"You're seeing waves comin' and going," Signar said without turning. "Nothing more than that!"

Still, I shaded my eyes and watched where Rhalgorn pointed. For a long moment, there was nothing. Then, of a sudden, three of the sandbars dropped completely beneath the surface. A line of small hairs marched up the back of my neck. "Signar—he is right. *Some*thing is happening out there."

"Damn me," growled the Vikonen, "not you too, Aldair?"

"And also me," put in Thareesh. I had not seen him come up behind us. "I am afraid the Stygiann is not seeing things. And whatever is there, I do not believe it is a sandbar."

With a scornful glance at us all, Signar stalked across the bridge and grudgingly studied the sea. "Like sailin' with a pack of children," he muttered, "jumping at every—" Suddenly, the words stuck in his throat. His big Vikonen jaw fell open and his eyes went wide. All about us, an enormous gray mass rolled heavily out of the sea. In the blink of an eye, it seemed as if the dark muddy floor of the ocean itself had risen up to meet us.

We stood there, frozen in our boots. Then Signar-Haldring came alive and leaped to the deck above, howling orders to the crew. Suddenly, seamen swarmed about the decks and into the rigging, like a nest of angry ants stirred with a stick. The *Ahzir* shuddered, came near dead in her wake, and turned straight for deep water. There was no time to imagine what was out there—clearly, it was something none of us cared to meet. "Signar!" I yelled above the din.

"We'll make it," he shouted back, "there's still a way open to deep water!"

Scurrying to a rope ladder, I climbed far enough to see ahead. The thing was moving slowly, sending blind patches of itself to seek us out. It was an awesome thing to behold. Neither liquid nor solid but something in between, it looked all the world like a great mass of porridge come to life. This was no reasoning creature, I was sure, but some blind, groping horror with only one grim purpose—to find the thing that had dared disturb its rest. It was all around us now, ahead, astern—

Creator's Eyes, the crew we'd sent in the longboat—! I searched the sea, but of course they were gone. They'd had no chance at all against the creature.

A shout went up from the bow and I jumped to the deck and ran forward. Rhalgorn and Thareesh had ranged our strength to port and starboard on the forward decks. Warriors poured one volley of missiles after another into the thing, javelins and arrows soaked in pitch and set afire. Wherever a missile struck, the beast quivered and shrank away from the terrible heat. The crew waved their arms about and cheered, though I am sure they knew there were not enough missiles in all the legions of Rhemia to stay the creature long.

It moved steadily in upon us, swallowing the sea in its path. Still, Signar stood firm on the bridge, urging the crew to catch every breath of wind in our sails. Suddenly, it seemed as if the gods of Vikonea themselves had heard his plea, for the canvas snapped like a whip and a fair breeze near lifted us off the waters. The crew howled, shook their weapons at the sea-thing, and the *Ahzir* surged hungrily for blue water.

In a single minute more, we would have surely been clear and away, but this was not to be. Fortune, who had taken us in her favor only moments before, suddenly looked aside. And in that moment the thing rose like a great wall to fill our path, and cut us from the sea.

Nineteen

It is easy to imagine that others may meet with some disaster, but no one truly believes he is personally at the end of his days—even when all the porridge in the world threatens to swallow his vessel. Thus, while despair touched every being aboard for a brief moment, we pulled ourselves together and rallied to our posts. As Rhalgorn said in passing, dying with sword in hand was one thing—being eaten by a soup was something else again. He was right. I could scarcely imagine a more unseemly way to go.

The sea-thing swelled and grew before our eyes; now it was no more than a dozen meters away on either side, and coming closer by the minute. Signar put a halt to our fruitless volley of missiles. Instead, he sent a party aft to quickly strip the decks and bring long planks of timber to the bow. There, he spread pitch on the ends of every piece, set them afire, and picked our strongest Vikonen warriors to heave them onto the growing mass. This was much more successful than arrows and spears, for the timbers lay where they fell and burned fiercely. The sea-beast writhed and shuddered, trying desperately to rid itself of the terrible heat that ate its flesh away. As we'd guessed, the thing was truly one vast creature, for it clearly felt the effect of our missiles on every part of its body.

"We're makin' some headway," said Signar, brushing his arm where a cinder had seared the fur, "but it ain't much, and we can't keep this kind of business goin' much longer. We're near out of pitch already, an' I'm damned if I'll toss the whole ship at that monster!"

Thareesh swept his arm from port to starboard. "What we are doing up front has no effect on the rest of it," he said grimly. "Look there—it'll be all over us in a moment, Aldair!"

I turned to Signar. "Get some of your fire tossers aft, quickly."

"Aldair, we can't keep—"

"Keep what—tearing up the *Ahzir*? Creator's Eyes, Signar, what difference does it make if we don't *stop* the thing? Do it!" Signar gave me a sour look and ran for the bow. I pulled Thareesh aside and told him to direct the action at the stern, then looked about for Rhalgorn. He was portside, breaking up the decking. I took him from that and led him to a corner of the bridge. "This fire tossing is only putting things off," I told him. "We could burn every ship in the Rhemian, Vikonen, and Nicean fleets and the damned thing would still be on us."

"This is so," Rhalgorn agreed, "but try to tell that to Signar."

"Signar can see his own death in the offing, but not the *Ahzir's*. It is the one great failing of ships' captains. Reason will come to him soon enough, but that's of no great help at the moment."

"Aldair," he said soberly, "what *is* of great help at the moment?"

"Good. You see the truth and know it for what it is, old friend." I gripped his arm firmly. "Unless the gods take a hand, this whole sorry business will be over before the sun is down. Am I right in this? Do you see another way?"

Rhalgorn shook his head. "I'd gladly argue if I could. It is over, Aldair. There is nothing else for it."

"There is one thing," I told him. "We can go down as warriors, and we will. You and Thareesh have every sword and war-axe in the armory brought amidships, and put in proper hands. The thing'll have to haul itself aboard to get to us—when it does, we'll ring the rails and meet it as best we can."

"It sounds like a noble stand indeed," said Rhalgorn, "until one remembers it is against a bowl of soup."

"Perhaps. But it is better than *not* standing against a bowl of soup."

"I suppose you are right."

From the bridge, we watched Vikonen warriors toss one firebrand after another at the sea-thing. If Signar-Haldring knew his cause was lost, he failed to show it, and his strength gave others courage to hold their ground. The creature still writhed and backed away from our missiles, but the ship was making little headway against it. We could no longer use our sails, for they would carry us right into the thing. Soon, our oars would be next to useless as well—the sea was fast disappearing on either side.

I turned to face Rhalgorn. "There is one more matter between us," I said. "I had better say this now, for there may not be another time for it. I do not imagine being eaten by this thing will be a very pleasant way to go. I—do not intend to put Corysia through that."

He looked at me, and nodded understanding.

"If anything should happen . . . if for—some reason I am not at the right place at the right time. . . ."

Rhalgorn stared at the deck. "It will be done, Aldair." There was more on his mind, but he left the words unsaid and hurried away, shouting for Thareesh.

I wondered where Corysia might be, and followed him forward. I did not wish to be far from her now. Though I could scarcely bear to think about it, I knew when the time came the will would find its way to my hand, and I would do it. I was appalled to find that such a thing could be—that in my heart she was dead to me already.

I saw her ahead with Signar, smearing pitch on scraps of timber and passing them hurriedly to another. She glanced up and caught my eye. I looked away, fearful and ashamed. How could I face her now? She would take one good look at me, and know. Quickly, I turned aside and started aft, making my way between the oarsmen. Halfway to the stern, a Niciean crewman leaped from his post and blundered into my path. Before he could send us both to the deck, I grabbed his shoulders and brought him to a halt. He shook me off, then saw who I was. "M-Master Aldair!" His eyes were wide with fear. All he could do was point dumbly down the length of his oar. I looked at him, then followed his trembling hand. My stomach turned over and the taste of bile rose to my throat. The end of the fellow's oar had disappeared in a mass of wet, gray flesh; pale fingers of the thing curled about its length and groped blindly for the *Ahzir*. Signar stomped up behind us and brushed us both aside. He ripped the oar from its lock and tossed it to the sea. The creature hungrily sucked it below the surface. Cupping big hands about his mouth, the Vikonen bellowed an order. Crewmen to port and starboard quickly raised their oars—three more had already been grasped by the sea-thing and we dropped them over the side.

Rhalgorn shouted from the bow and pointed. Signar and I turned to hear but his words were lost—the *Ahzir* suddenly creaked and shuddered beneath us and near rose out of the water. Signar went pale under his fur and groped for a hold. "Creator's Eyes, Aldair, it's *under* us!" My feet gave way and I reached for his belt and held on. The Vikonen pulled me to him and scrambled amidships for higher ground. The ship heaved again, and listed to port. A crewman screamed near the stern; out of the corner of my eye I saw another slide along the deck and into the sea. Corysia! I glanced wildly about, searching the decks. *"Corysia!"*

I heard my name above the din and jerked around. She was behind me, clinging to a railing by the bridge. When she saw me, she let go and started for me across the slanting decks.

"Corysia, *no!*" It was too late. Scrambling to my feet, I ran for her, knowing I'd never make it. The ship quivered again and she went to her knees. Surprise crossed her features, turning quickly to horror as she realized what was happening. She clawed for something to stop her but there was nothing. Her eyes watched me helplessly all the way, and I knew she was gone. "Corysia! *Corysia!*"

A blur of gray came out of nowhere, moving past me straight for the sloping bridge. Rhalgorn gave a single bound and leaped, stretching his gaunt frame to the limit. For a terrible second, they hung there over nothing, inches apart— then Rhalgorn pulled Corysia to his chest and slammed his boots hard against the railing. Wood splintered, and the Stygiann's feet went out from under him. Corysia screamed as something pale and gray snaked out of the water and slapped at Rhalgorn's boots. He kicked out savagely, holding Corysia to him and clinging desperately to the broken rail with the crook of his arm.

I was nearly on them, blade already in hand. Signar passed me in one giant step to scoop them both in his burly arms. The thing had Rhalgorn in its grip and wouldn't let go. Signar tugged with all his might and the Stygiann's face contorted in pain. I hacked again and again at the dark wet tentacle of flesh. It was tough and stringy and strong as good armor— not at all like the porridge it appeared.

"Aldair—*hurry!*" groaned Signar. He gritted his teeth, muscles tensing like cords of rope across his back. My arm was near numb from hacking—still the creature hung on. For a brief moment, I wondered if I'd have to take Rhalgorn's leg to set him free. No, damn me, I would not! We'd all likely die here before the sun was down, but I vowed the Stygiann would go with both his legs intact.

Shouting the worst Venicii curse I could remember, I tossed the sword behind me and jerked Signar's war-axe from his belt. Normally, I could scarcely lift the great weapon, but it seemed no more than a toy to me now. I wielded the axe with all the strength I could muster. Again— And again— Suddenly, the terrible flesh parted and Signar-Haldring fell back, nearly losing his burdens. An awesome stench rose from the severed limb and it writhed back into the sea.

Something slapped against my shoulder and I clung to it gratefully. Glancing up at the sloping deck I saw the stout seaman Stumbaucius looping the rope securely about the mast. He nodded without expression, then hurried on his way. Signar and I started Rhalgorn and Corysia up the line, then quickly followed after.

Corysia gave a little cry and flung her arms about me. "Aldair! Oh, Aldair, I thought—I thought—"

"Corysia. It's all right." Hot tears scalded my shoulder. I held her a moment, then gently pushed her away. She looked at me, but I busied myself with a length of cord at my belt. Before she could speak I looped it quickly around her, binding her securely to the mast.

"Aldair—" She pulled away, puzzlement showing through the tears. "What's—that for?"

"That's to make sure it doesn't happen again. It's all right, Corysia."

"Stop saying that!" she snapped angrily.

I couldn't look at her. "You'll—be safe, Corysia."

"Safe!" She strained against her bonds. "*Damn* you, Aldair, I'm not a child." Her voice was dreadfully calm. "I know what is happening here. I can hold a sword as well as any other."

I turned away from her. "Aldair, *look* at me!"

"Rhalgorn—can you stand?"

"The leg is fine," he said dully. "A little longer than the

other, perhaps. That is a fairly strong soup, Aldair." He made a face and pulled himself up.

"Rhalgorn," Corysia pleaded, "will *you* listen? I don't—"

"Lady," Rhalgorn turned on her, "do not be in such a great hurry to die. There is plenty of time for that!"

She reeled back, visibly shaken by his words, for there was a strong bond between them. Rhalgorn turned quickly and stalked away, before she could see there was anything but anger in his eyes. I had no more courage than the Stygiann, and followed on his heels. She shouted at my back, but I didn't listen. I would be with her again soon enough. When it was time, I would know where to find her.

Before Rhalgorn and I could reach the bow the ship heaved again and suddenly righted itself, sending us all to the decks. A few crewmen cheered at this, but Signar's shout from the stern told us no great victory had occurred. Clmbing to the bridge again we peered aft, and saw the sea-creature had made a sudden assault on our rear. If there was ever a time to lose courage, this, indeed, was the moment. The stern of the *Ahzir* was near covered in a mass of wet, gray flesh. It oozed through the railing with a hundred terrible fingers and crawled steadily along the decks. Signar and a handful of warriors stood against it—Thareesh led a dozen more from amidships, Rhalgorn and I on their heels.

I have seen more than one grim battle in my time, but none like the one we fought there on the narrow stern of the *Ahzir*. No great war-cries shook the air; no awful din of weapons or clash of horse and armor. Instead, an almost eerie silence covered the ship, broken only by the dull rhythm of sword and axe on near unyielding flesh.

The sea-creature could not be stopped.

We knew this, but we could not simply toss our weapons aside and let it take us. We would fight until we could fight no more. There is little else for a warrior to do.

The dark carpet of flesh surged endlessly out of the sea, forcing us back until the stern was nearly covered in its mass. We fought until our arms grew numb; the haft of my sword turned red with the blood of my own raw hands. Beside me, a Nicean staggered back and dropped his weapon. Thareesh reached down and jerked him to his feet with a long string of Nicean curses.

"We are lost!" cried the warrior.

"By all the gods, you are *alive!*" hissed Thareesh. "Pick up your blade and fight!"

A shout from amidships brought me about. Just below the bridge, a damp tongue of matter slid up the hull and onto the decks. A lone Vikonen stood against it. I ran to his side and yelled for a crew to help. No one heard. It was only one small battle in the midst of the war. Another cry from starboard . . . a shout from the bow. Of a sudden, the thing was everywhere, and we were lost for certain.

I'll be coming for you soon, Corysia, for I will not have you see the end of this!

The ship groaned. Timber cracked beneath my boots. For the first time, it occurred to me the sea-thing didn't *have* to take every inch of the *Ahzir*—long before that, we would sink under the weight of its mass. Hurrying to the bridge, I looked aft. The stern was completely smothered in gray flesh. In a moment, the bow would go as well, for the creature had flowed across the deck from port to starboard and joined itself amidships. The crewmen there saw this, and dropped their weapons in fear. Some leaped the river of flesh and ran to the bridge—others climbed the mast and scurried into the rigging. There was no safety there, but they would live a moment longer.

It was time. . . .

I had decided how to do it. Simply come up behind the mast and drive the blade home quickly. It had to be this way. If I faced her once, looked into her eyes . . .

The short Venicii knife was in my hand. It was cold as ice. Hot as new iron.

No!

It would be over. She would never see the worst of it.

Corysia!

I shut all thoughts of her away—

Corysia, forgive me!

—raised the blade, and brought it down swiftly.

Thunder shook the *Ahzir*. My legs gave way and sent me sprawling to the deck. The knife fell from my hand and clattered on wood. I glanced up, saw Corysia. She looked at me, stared at the knife at her feet. Her eyes went wide with understanding.

"Aldair—oh, *Aldair!*"

The thunder came again. It rolled out of the east, bright as a smaller sun, flashing across the bow of the *Ahzir*. I got to my feet, tore the cord from Corysia and brought her into my arms. She spoke, but her words were lost. I held her away and stared at the sky. Signar staggered up beside us. "Great gods, what in all the hells is *that!*"

It came from far astern, now, a shimmering ball of quicksilver moving just above the sea. It passed us with a roar, and the *Ahzir* shuddered in its wake. It was there—then it was gone.

"Isn't *any*thing can move as fast as that!" said the Vikonen.

"Something can."

"Look!" cried Corysia. The thing slowed, far ahead of the ship, made a quick arc to port and settled just above our bow. Closer, I could tell it was a great and shining sphere, its sides awash in light too bright to look upon. It hung there a moment, flashing in the sun, then slowly turned to starboard. As it passed, a tiny circle opened in its belly and a beam of pale blue light winked down to touch the sea-thing.

The beast quivered, writhed in sudden agony. Great clouds of nauseous steam rose from its tattered flesh. We could almost hear its howls of pain as the blue column of light burned its life away. The *Ahzir* trembled; I grabbed Corysia and clung to the mast. The golden sphere made a wide circle around us, wreaking havoc in its path.

All about us, the sea-thing began to change. The tough, unyielding flesh we'd battled moments before quivered and shook uncontrollably, as if a thousand different creatures were within it, fighting to tear themselves free. Of a sudden, whatever held it together gave way, and it began to come apart before our eyes. Gray turned sickly white; one pale slab of matter after another slid from the mass, and dropped into the sea. Soon, all that was left of this terrible creature were patches of lifeless jelly about our decks, and a milky film upon the water.

For a long moment no one dared to breathe aboard the *Ahzir*. It is no easy thing to move from the living to the dead, then back again in the blink of an eye. We could scarce begin to fathom the thing that had crawled upon our decks and nearly brought us to disaster. Now, we could no more easily imagine it was gone.

And if that were not enough, there was still another wonder

to behold. It hovered above our mast, just beyond the bow. We stared, unable to move. What could it be? If it had not appeared, we would now be dead beneath the waters. Yet, I feared it greatly—for who but Man could fashion such a marvel?

It loomed above us, vast and silent as a sun come down to earth. Then it turned about, moved slowly out to sea, and sped like a ball of fire into the heavens.

In that brief moment, I knew the madness of this day was not yet over. For as it turned, we clearly saw its other side: Etched upon that golden sphere was a perfect likeness of the *Ahzir al'Rhaz,* broad sails full upon the wind. . . .

Twenty

I am told the day dawned bright and clear following our encounter with the sea-creature. This may be so. It is a time I can scarce remember, for I shut myself away from the world and spoke to no one. Brooding and self-pity are not in my nature, and I have seldom fallen prey to such business. This time, however, when the dark cloak of despair descended upon me, I lacked the will to toss it aside. I wept, cursed myself soundly, and flailed myself with guilt. I also drank a great deal of wine and barley beer. This is a disastrous mixture at best, and little of it stayed on my stomach.

All in all, it was a shameful waste of time, and when it was over I felt no better for it. I ruined a good suit of clothes, stank up my cabin and came to a painful decision. In truth, it was a decision I would have reached without the weeping and wailing that came with it.

I had no desire to face my companions. Still, I could not live forever in my cabin, locked away with the odor of despair. When I finally emerged on deck, the day was near an end. The sun was lost in a fiery wall of clouds over the southern continent, and the sea was red as brass. We were far from shore, circling in safe water. Signar had wisely kept us underway to let a good wind stir across the decks. Other than that, we were going nowhere at all, for the Vikonen had no course to follow. He was waiting for the brave leader of our expedition to get his wits about him.

"It is good to see you again," he said, coming up behind. "At least, I *think* it is," he added, sniffing the air about me.

I didn't look at him. "A little stale barley beer never hurt a Vikonen," I said bluntly. "If the smell offends you, Signar, stand somewhere else."

He held his tongue a moment, and I could hear him scratching his muzzle thoughtfully. "*Stale* ain't exactly the way I'd put it," he said finally. "*Used* is more to the point."

"Used, then. The remedy's still the same. If you don't care for it—"

"Now *look*, Aldair—" He grabbed my arm and turned me roughly about. "It's not your smell concerns me an' you damn well know it! How you are yourself is what I'm thinking on!"

I stared at him. "And how do you think I am, Signar? How should I be?"

"That ain't for me to say, but this isn't it, for sure."

"How many did we lose?"

He went blank a moment. "What?"

"You heard me plain enough. How many?"

He made a face and looked to the decking. "Six. Two in the longboat, four to—to that whatever is was."

I laughed, and stepped past him to the railing. "Six? Why, that's not bad at all, is it? Considering what I lost at Rhemia, or the two *ships* full up the river in Merrkia."

"You want to blame yourself for all that, go right ahead and do it," he said flatly.

"Well now who's *likely* to be blaming?" I asked him. "You? Rhalgorn? Thareesh? Who brought us here? I'm getting somewhat weary of all the fates and god-dreams and other mysterious powers that are supposed to be floating around somewhere making things happen. They don't, Signar. In the end, it's we who choose one path or another. And the paths I've chosen so far have brought us nothing but disaster!"

Signar frowned and searched the sea. "Didn't any of us figure it'd come to this, Aldair," he said gently. "—That we'd be losin' one handful of folks after another. You're right enough in that. On the other hand, there's not one among us didn't know what he was getting into. If these fates of yours or whatever'd wanted to make it easy, why, I reckon they'd just drop the secrets of Man right in our laps, like a fine keg of ale."

"True," I told him, "but they have not chosen to do this. So it all comes back to one thing, doesn't it? You said it yourself: who would ever have dreamed it would cost so many lives? You didn't. I didn't. Certainly, the warriors and crewmen I've sent to their deaths never imagined what this hapless voyage would cost them."

The Vikonen said nothing for a long moment. He gripped

the railing in his big hands, muttering to himself. Finally, he turned and faced me squarely. "We've been through much together, Aldair, and if I can't talk to you straight, why, I can't to any other. I know why you're talking like this and I don't blame you for it. But that don't change the fact that what you're saying is plain damn foolishness! There just isn't no other way to put it!"

He surprised me, and I guess it showed. "Hold on," he said, "I ain't finished yet. Just listen and hear the end of it. You've done a lot of talkin' about losing this many and losing that many, and you haven't said a thing about how many is *too* many."

"What?" His words puzzled me.

"*Too* many, Aldair." He laid a finger on my chest. "If we was startin' off this voyage tomorrow from Raadnir, and you knew for certain we'd find just what we were looking for— how many lives would you spend to get it? One? A dozen? Would you give yourself? Me? Corysia? Half the crew—or all of them?" He shook his great head. "You see what I'm saying, Aldair? *If what we're after ain't worth every life aboard and then some—then it sure as hell isn't worth even one!*"

He was right, of course. During the darkest hours of our ventures, this very thought had been my strength. If I had not believed this, I could never have found the courage to risk so much for a prize that seemed ever out of reach, always past tomorrow's far horizon. What Signar could not see was that his words meant nothing to me now. I had gone as far as I could go, and I could go no farther. How many lives could I give to reach our goal? For the first time since our quest began, I could truthfully answer this question. *Too many was one more.* Even if it meant for certain we would break the chains of history and free the world from the terrible legacy of Man. I would gladly give myself for this. But I did not have it in me to spend the life of another.

At supper, and after, I talked to the others. Their arguments were much the same as Signar's. Could I abandon our quest so easily? No, I could not. It tore the very fabric of my soul to do so. It left me hollow, empty, without purpose. Then how could I bring myself to do such a thing? Because I could do nothing else. Did every warrior who'd died for our cause give his life for nothing, then? Yes, I said. For little or nothing.

All the more reason to see that no more did the same.

Thareesh felt we should be encouraged by the appearance of the silver vessel that had saved us from the sea-thing. "Even the crew has taken heart," he argued. "They think it a most favorable omen, Aldair. And while I do not have the superstitious nature of a seaman, it is hard to disagree with them on this."

"Why?" I asked him.

"Why?" Thareesh seemed startled by such a question. "Do you not find it *mildly* interesting that such a wondrous device just *happened* to appear at a most propitious time, Aldair? And that it *happened* to bear the likeness of the *Ahzir al'Rhaz* on its side? That it exists at all is miracle enough, but the fact that—"

"Thareesh—" I stopped him rudely. "I am afraid I did not make myself quite clear. I am not questioning the wonder of the thing. I saw it. It was there. Though *why* it was there and where it came from I can't imagine. And neither can *you*, Thareesh—which is the point of the matter. Do you know why you and the crew and everyone else aboard this ship think that—that whatever it is—is a *good omen*? Because you want it to be, that's why! You said it yourself and I'm damned if it's not so. Every last one of you are thinking like superstitious sailors!"

Thareesh stood abruptly. His eyes went dark, but he held his anger. "I don't think this is a good time for us to talk, Aldair. Perhaps later. . . ."

"No," I told him. "Hear what I have to say, and don't think less of me because of my manners, or what I've become since our encounter with the sea-thing. I am the same person—and I am not the same. I do not see things as I did before. I can no longer send warriors to their deaths on the strength of dreams and omens. Each time I have done this, someone dies. Kenyarsha, Rhemia, Merrkia—and now Amazon. *I* brought us here, Thareesh. Because it *came* to me that this was the thing to do—that some great power or other guided us to this place. That here, we would find an answer to what we seek. I do not have to tell you what we found."

"And because we met the sea-thing, you are certain you were wrong." He shook his head fiercely. "That is not sound reason speaking, Aldair."

"*Reason?*" I stood and faced him squarely. "Creator's Eyes, old friend, reason has nothing to do with this! Perhaps the secret we seek does lie up that river. I have no idea. I know I will *not* spend lives to find out!"

The Nicean's shoulders fell. "And what if it *is* there, Aldair? What if you are wrong in casting omens aside—what if the appearance of the strange craft was meant to point the way? Can you really ignore that possibility? Can you stop now, this close to our goal? The sea-thing that stood in our way is dead—"

"Is it?" I swept an arm across the sea. "Can you look out there and tell me it is gone, because you cannot see it?"

Thareesh flushed. "I *saw* it die, Aldair!"

"Perhaps you did," I said. "And perhaps there is another. And another—"

"*Damn* me," he said, clenching his fists around the railing. "You would argue the sun comes up in the west, Aldair!"

I reached over and laid a hand upon his shoulder. "I think you are right, Thareesh. Perhaps you will meet a better, more agreeable Aldair in the morning. I have few good friends in this most unfriendly world of ours. It would not be overly wise to anger them all at once."

The Nicean brought himself up stiffly. "Your companions will not turn away from you because they disagree with what you say, Aldair."

"No," I told him, "I am certain, after all this time, they will not. At one time or another, I have given you all good reason to do so."

In truth, I was not a "better Aldair" on the morrow. I did not try to antagonize my companions. It simply turned out that way. They sought me out, one by one, to bring me to my senses. They presented a number of sound, practical reasons why I should change my mind and continue our quest. I agreed with them all. I told them they were right and I was wrong. In the end, however, I merely sent them away more disgruntled than ever. For I could not bring myself to say that I would risk a one of them for all the secrets of Man.

They were understanding—or tried to be. But their eyes told me what they were thinking, and I was truly ashamed to face them. For neither Rhalgorn, Corysia, Thareesh, nor Signar-Haldring would put to words the question that was in all their minds: if Aldair will not lead us farther, where are we to go? As I had so wisely told the seaman Barthius, there is only one goal worth seeking in a world that is falling to ruin. Now, I myself had turned aside from that goal.

Even Corysia could not see what had really happened to me. She could not understand that I had not simply abandoned my quest—that I truly had no say in the matter. I could no more send another companion to die than a fellow whose hands are bound can drink a mug of ale.

More than once during this time, I remembered a story I had heard as a child. It concerned a very brave warrior who went off to battle, and returned to find his village destroyed. His home was gone. His wife and children and all his friends had been put to the sword. The warrior wept, grieved for all he had lost, then set about to seek revenge upon his enemies. He polished his armor, honed his weapons and raged silently against his foes.

Weeks went by and still the warrior did not go to battle. He found dents in his armor. His weapons were never as sharp as they should be. His blouse and his boots needed patching. In the end, the warrior found that no matter how he tried he could not get beyond the bounds of his village. He could get that far, and no farther. He was not a coward. He did not fear death. Something had simply died inside him—he had lost too much, and could lose no more. Finally, his enemies returned to the village and found him there, sitting on a stone. Try as he might, he could not raise a finger to protect himself.

I had never understood this story before.

Twenty-one

We could argue all we liked about what we might do, and where we might go—but the truth of the matter was we were going nowhere at all until the *Ahzir* was in shape again. The ship was indeed a shambles. The decking was nearly gone. Half the railing was missing, and a great many timbers from the bridge and below decks had been ripped from their places to fight the sea-thing. We looked a great deal more like an old abandoned scow than the finest, fastest ship afloat.

Worst of all, of course, was the damage that *didn't* show. Signar had collected a list of problems he sourly divided into two categories: Things that needed to be fixed immediately, and things that *must* be fixed before that. "We don't need nothin' a good shipyard an' about two months work wouldn't fix," he said darkly.

We were seaworthy, he admitted, but just barely. We could circle about slowly in a good flat sea, but he paled at the thought of facing strong winds or rough water. "We could make it across a fair duckpond without sinking," he announced. "I ain't guaranteeing more'n that."

It was a wonder, truly we were still afloat at all. Ships were not built to be crushed, pummeled, stood on end and near eaten whole by sea monsters. It is a credit to those who built the *Ahzir* that she had not snapped amidships and gone to the bottom.

For several days, we spent our time making what repairs we could. These efforts were limited, at best, for we had no spare timber or pitch, having used both these items in plenty against the sea-thing. Thus, to shore up one weak spot in the hull, it was necessary to steal the materials from another. Soon, we were in danger of *causing* more leaks than we repaired.

"It don't much matter whether you *want* to put ashore or

not," Signar told me. "There isn't any choice in the matter, Aldair. We either find a good harbor and put things right with the *Ahzir,* or we leave her here to rot."

"We could—look for another river, couldn't we?" I suggested, knowing as I spoke this was clearly out of reason.

Signar gave me a long, steady look. "I know your feelings," he said, "and I'll respect 'em as best I can. But the answer is *no,* and you know that as well as I do. This Amazon of yours is right square in front of us, and I don't have to tell you how many leagues it goes on either side. We haven't got *time* to find some other river. We'll be damn lucky if we get upriver *any*where 'fore we sink right to the bottom."

He was right, and I could not argue the point. Neither could I put aside the almost unreasoning fear that plagued me at the thought of sailing up that great river. What was *happening* to me, I wondered. Not for the first time, I seriously questioned my motives. Was I ready to abandon our quest because I could no longer stomach the death of others, or was it something else entirely? Maybe I was worried about myself—not my companions.

I have never thought of myself as either cowardly or excessively brave. Like most who grow up in the warrior trade, I feel I am somewhere in between. I have stood and fought when it would have been wiser to turn and run—but I am not sure this can properly be called bravery. A soldier fights and holds his ground because there is no place else to go. There is an enemy before him bent on cleaving him in half with axe or sword. If he runs, he stands a good chance of getting a weapon or two up his backside. Though many warriors might disagree, I am inclined to think bravery is simply a very practical approach to the fighting business.

Thus, I do not believe it was a personal kind of fear that haunted my days and made me a stranger to my companions. This was something else again. It was a fear I could neither face nor fight, for it would not come forth and show itself. It was there, though, for certain. Like the warrior in the fable, I could go so far, and no farther.

How the gods must have laughed at my feeble efforts to set their will aside! If I did not wish to follow my quest upriver, why, they would get me there some other way. And if I balked at *those* efforts, I could squat like a turnip on the *Ahzir,* and watch it sink beneath me.

At least, there was work to be done a'plenty—good hard labor under a boiling sun. I welcomed it gladly, for it kept the hands a great deal busier than the mind. I had found a special task for myself, one peculiarly suited to my race. Neither Vikonen, Niciean nor Stygiann folk are overly fond of the water. They will sail upon it, and drink it if they have to, but they have no desire to actually get *in* it. They will swim to keep from drowning, but cannot imagine a creature might find it enjoyable to splash about for the pure pleasure of it.

"Most unseemly," sniffed Rhalgorn, "and likely bad for the health to boot."

"Stygianns would do well to practice the art of bathing," I told him. "How do you think the Venicii find them in the dark—though our eyes are not nearly as sharp as your own?"

Rhalgorn scratched his muzzle thoughtfully. "I will answer your question with another, Aldair. How do you imagine the sharks that flourish in these waters find a swimming Venicii warrior? At a guess, I'd say they hear their fine fat bodies cavorting about from a league or so away."

"I am not concerned about sharks," I told him, though this was not entirely true. "They are always around, but they seldom bother anything that does not bother them first."

"That is a good, sound philosophy, Aldair. I trust the sharks have heard it, too."

"Do be careful," said Corysia, laying a hand on mine. "If you see *anything* down there. . . ."

"I will," I assured here. "And I will bring you a fine shell or two to add to your collection."

What I said about the nature of sharks is true, for the most part. They are fierce, voracious creatures, but generally keep their distance. Nevertheless, they have an ignoble reputation, and we never worked in the water without lookouts posted in tthe rigging, and armed warriors stationed in the stern.

There were three in the work party—Barthius, Stumbaucius and myself. Barthius, as usual, was somewhat surly and resentful, but he was by far the best diver among us. I praised him for his work, but I fear this merely offended him all the more. Stumbaucius was his usual, reliable self—not overly graceful beneath the water, but willing and able.

It was hard, challenging work. A pin had splintered in the rudder, making it difficult for Signar to hold a course at any great speed. On dry land, it would have been a simple job to remove the damaged part and substitute another. Underwater, it was a tiring, demanding task. We could work only a short time without coming up for air; most of our strength was wasted going down and coming up again. Nevertheless, we managed to get the shattered pin loose and in the hands of a craftsman above, and this fellow quickly shaped another to match it. All that remained was the awesome task of pounding it in place again underwater.

"Take a care," warned Signar. "It can be neither too loose nor too tight, or we will be in worse trouble than we were. If it is too loose it will not swell to fit—too tight, and it'll swell and lock and likely shatter the mechanism."

I lay on the deck listening to him, gasping—so to speak—like a fish out of water. "You will have to trust us," I told him, "unless you care to inspect the job yourself."

"I think that would be the wisest course," Rhalgorn said thoughtfully. "It is never a good idea to trust boat-things to amateurs."

Signar glared at him. "You'd like that, wouldn't you, now?"

"It would be most interesting," said Rhalgorn. "I have often wondered whether a Vikonen would float in water, or sink to the bottom."

"They float," Signar told him. "But I ain't real sure about Stygianns. We could find out quick enough."

For myself, I would have given much to see them *both* paddling about behind the *Ahzir*. There are many bizarre creatures in the sea, but none could match the two of them.

The world beneath the waves is a strange and beautiful place indeed. In clear, tropical seas, one can see a great distance, and it is easy to imagine there is truly no water there at all—that you are hanging suspended in some green and magical land. The *Ahzir* floated serenely, three fathoms above a white sandy bottom. There were few creatures about, though we occasionally saw a school of brilliantly colored fish dart about in the distance. Once, a pair came nearly up to the rudder and watched us curiously. They were yellow striped in blue, and flat as a frying pan. After a moment, they turned and darted away.

As soon as I tried the new pin, I was certain it was much too large to fit properly. Bringing it back to the surface, I

tossed it to the decks with instructions to pare it down a bit.
Stumbaucius bobbed up beside me, then Barthius. "Tell him
not to whittle the thing down to a nub," he said crossly, "or
we'll have to be startin' all over again—sir," he added quickly.

"I did," I told him. "We will take it slow and easy, until
we get it right."

"Keep an eye open down there," called Thareesh. "One of
the lookouts says he spotted something."

"What?"

"He couldn't say. Some kind of activity to starboard."

"Most likely a school of fish," said Stumbaucius.

"Or something *eatin'* a school of fish," Barthius muttered
darkly.

I looked at them both. "We can stop awhile, if either of you
cares to. It makes no difference to me."

"If it's all the same to you, sir," said Stumbaucious, "let's
get it over and done with."

"Barthius?"

Barthius shrugged, but cast a scornful eye at his shipmate.
Signar tossed me the newly whittled pin and I looked it over,
then nodded to the decks. It looked as if it would do the job.
Barthius reached out for it and I gave it to him, along with
the heavy wooden mallet we used for a hammer. He took a
deep breath, and plunged beneath the surface. After a long
moment, he was back again, spitting water. "It'll do," he said.
"Just give it a couple of good whacks, Master Aldair. I already got it in place." I nodded, took the hammer, and went
below.

Recalling Barthius' eagerness to get out of the water, I
inspected the job carefully. Sure enough, though, he was right.
The peg fit perfectly, and when it swelled, would stay snugly
in place.

It is not easy to hammer underwater, and after a few strokes
I was out of air and swimming for the surface. Stumbaucius
reached for the hammer but I shook my head. "I've got it
going—I'll finish it off and you can take a look at it." Taking
an extra good breath, I pushed off from the hull and went
back below.

Having been at the job all day, I discovered I could stay
down a good deal longer than I had in the beginning. Like
any other skill, it takes some getting used to. Thus, I was sur-

prised and pleased to find the job was nearly done while I still had a bit of air to go. One more tap or two—

Suddenly, something jerked me away from the rudder and pulled the hammer from my hand. I turned, startled, and found Stumbaucius floating there behind me. He clutched my arm with one hand, gesturing wildly with the other. I pulled away, wondering what had come over the fellow. He grabbed for me again, pointing desperately at the sandy floor below. I looked—and nearly sucked in a mouthful of water. A dozen dark shapes glided swiftly across the ocean floor, stirring a fine sandy wake behind them.

I didn't need to look twice. Turning about, I followed Stumbaucius, churning for the surface. Out of the corner of my eye I could see a hail of spears and arrows cutting the water behind us. I broke the surface, gulped in air, and saw a line snake out from the decks above. I grabbed for it, missed. The hull was only a meter away and I made for it desperately. If I could scramble up the sides, get a fair hold—

Of a sudden, something black and shiny surged out of the sea and sent me sprawling. Then, a grip strong as iron took both my legs and jerked me beneath the water. . . .

Twenty-two

In one small corner of my mind, I wondered idly why it was not a great deal more painful to be eaten by a shark. I was scared near witless. My lungs were close to bursting—yet, strangely enough, I was still alive.

Glancing up, I saw the hull of the *Ahzir* far above, the sun dancing on the water around it. Then, that friendly sight disappeared as two dark shapes loomed up directly before me. Trailing between them was a bright, transparent—something. Like a jar turned upside down. Before I could blink, they thrust this thing over me and I was swallowed up inside. Creator's Eyes, I thought, they're not going to eat me themselves —they're *feeding* me to a friend!

My lungs burned. I flailed about blindly against my prison, clawing to get free. The world went black around me and I could hold my breath no longer. I opened my mouth and sucked water, praying the end would come quickly.

Water? Bewildered, I opened my mouth and breathed again. *Damn me, it wasn't water at all—it was air!* I wondered at this marvel for the small part of a second, then took a few more grateful breaths. It was not overly fresh and pure, smelling slightly fishy—but it was air, and that was good enough for me.

Confident that I was at least safe and secure for the moment, I inspected the thing around me. It was neither hard nor quite solid as I had first imagined, but soft and pliant to the touch. At its top, it was clear as glass, fading to a pale, milky purple farther down. I noted a ring of knobby protuberances at the level of my waist and reached out to touch them, thinking they'd be something stable to hold on to. I was still treading water up to my chest, and this was somewhat tiring.

At my touch, the glassy thing shuddered violently and squeezed me hard. Water rushed up from below and sent me

118

gasping. Finally, the thing quieted, and I could breathe again. Whatever it was, it did not care to be handled.

Suddenly, a face loomed up outside, appearing so quickly it near startled me out of my wits. For the first time, I got a good long look at one of my captors. Surprisingly enough, it appeared neither vicious nor frightening. There was intelligence and concern in its eyes, and I sensed, somehow, it meant me no harm. This was no shark as I had first imagined, for it looked all the world like a great porpoise. It had the long, graceful nose of its kind, and was sleek and black all over except for its white underbelly. It hung there a long moment, watching me. Then, it reached up slowly and placed a palm over the transparent creature, directly in front of my face.

I shrank back amazed. This was no ordinary porpoise at all, but another creation of Man! From the dark flippers at its sides grew a pair of perfectly usable hands, much like my own. Instinctively, I reached out and placed a hand against his. The wide mouth opened slightly in understanding. He spoke, then, and though I could not make out his words, I answered his greeting with my own.

From behind him, another dark form appeared and brought itself up beside us. It was a smaller creature than the first, and I decided it was a female. She looked at me curiously a moment, then spoke to her mate. They carried on a short conversation in high, shrill tones, gesturing first at me, then at the creature around me. Finally, the male turned and pointed at the fleshy knobs of the creature and nodded his great head. I was puzzled at this. Was he telling me it was all right to hold on to the things? I pointed, and reached out as if to touch them. Both he and the female nodded vigorously.

"No," I shook my head, "I'm tired of treading water in here—but not *that* tired."

The male started to speak, but the female stopped him. She moved up closer and placed her hands on the creature, talking to it in soothing tones. "It is all right," she seemed to say, "the being inside you means no harm."

All right, then, I decided. I would give it a try. After all, I could do no more than drown. Reaching out carefully with one hand, I touched the creature lightly. It jerked away slightly, but the female continued to gentle it. I gripped the fleshy knob more firmly. Then tried the other. Nothing happened. My new companions smiled at each other, then at me. As one, they turned and swam away to join their party.

Though I could not guess where it might be, the porpoise folk clearly had some destination in mind. We moved swiftly along, just above the ocean floor, slowed only by the creature who carried me in its belly. I had guessed, finally, it was some sort of giant jellyfish, tamed to do the bidding of its masters. It had no mind of its own, and would sometimes veer off in another direction until it was goaded back onto the proper path.

It was a long journey, and I had ample time to marvel at the wonders of the world beneath the sea. Great ridges of living coral loomed around us in a hundred startling colors. Fields of sea grass waved gently in an unseen breeze. Creatures I had never dreamed of swam all about. Once, we plunged into a veritable cloud of bright red fish, a school so large it seemed to fill the sea.

The air inside my creature was growing stale. I began to worry about this, but the porpoise folk had anticipated my needs. Twice before our trip was over we came to a stop to find a new creature waiting. The big male indicated by gestures that I should hold my breath and move from one source of air to another. This was a rather frightening experience, but I did it quickly and without question, having little choice in the matter.

For the first half of our journey we stayed in relatively shallow seas; the light from above was still bright and clear around us. Then, of a sudden, the white sandy floor gave way to darkness, and we plunged into an inky abyss. I had not been overly concerned before—there was air to breathe, and the friendliness of the porpoise folk was calmly reassuring. Now, the last reminder of my own world abruptly dropped away and I was seized by a cold, unreasoning fear. I was alone and helpless—I had no idea where my captors were taking me. How did I *know* they were really friendly? Just because they were taking great pains to keep me alive for the moment did *not* mean I was out of danger. *Suppose they were merely saving me for some greater horror to come!*

Though there was ample air to breathe, I suddenly felt trapped, crushed by the terrible weight of the sea. Cold sweat stood out upon my brow and stung my eyes. My chest was

bound in iron—I gasped for breath, clawed at the sides of my
prison. I *had* to get out—I could not stay in that place a moment longer!

Light blossomed around me, a deep unearthly blue. It lit
the pale sides of the sea creature and, an instant later, the
faces of the porpoise folk. They quickly thrust their hands
against the cold, transparent flesh—without thinking, I pressed
my palms against theirs. The moment we touched, all the fears
within me fell away. I was nearly overwhelmed by a feeling of
great peace and joy. I cried out; tears sprang to my eyes and
ran warmly down my cheeks. I loved the porpoise folk, the sea
around me, the strange creature that held me in its body and
gave me life. What a wonderful thing it was to be alive!

A moment later, the porpoise folk turned and disappeared
into the darkness, leaving a trail of bright bubbles dancing in
their wake. The pale blue lights stayed clustered around me,
and though the powerful sense of love and well being I'd experienced gently subsided, it did not vanish completely. For
the rest of our journey I felt secure and at peace with my sur-
roundings. . . .

Far ahead and below, a dim glow appeared in the depths
of the sea. Closer, I could tell it was a great cluster of ghost
lights, much like the ones that followed my oversized jellyfish.
There were a dozen different colors—cold blues and greens,
pale lemon yellows, reds the shade of a dying fire. I could not
imagine what they might be. Soon, however, we were sweeping down among them.

I held my breath and gripped the sides of the creature, staring at the sights around me. Clearly, this was the home of the
porpoise folk! Everywhere I looked there were hundreds,
thousands of them, streaming through the eerie light, bent on
errands I could scare imagine.

In moments, we were in the heart of a vast and beautiful
city, sweeping down one watery avenue after another. All
about us, graceful spires of coral rose from the floor of the
sea—faerie towers lost in the wavering heights. There were
high, impossibly delicate columns the color of lustrous pearl
. . . pink, spidery arches that would have crumbled in a second
on the land. I was greatly taken by this place, and thought it
put the ugly cities I had known to shame.

Somewhere near the center of the city, the porpoise folk

guided my sea-creature around a high, lavender structure and into a large, underwater courtyard. This long and narrow place was honeycombed with passageways from one end to the other. Some were lit by the ghost lights, others were dark as night. My friends chose one of the darker holes, and we plunged abruptly into the bowels of the city.

During this short trip, I lost all sense of direction, having no idea whether we were moving up, down or sideways. Then, just as I grew used to the darkness, the way ahead was suddenly bathed in dazzling light. Seconds later, to my great surprise, the sea creature slowed its pace and we bobbed to the *surface* of the water! Looking about, I saw we were in a small cavern carved from solid coral. The walls and ceiling of this place were alive with ghost lights; their brilliance lit the water with a million colored stars.

The porpoise folk were already there, circling about and calling out to one another in high, shrill whistles. The male swam up beside me and began chattering away excitedly, breathing in a most exaggerated manner. Clearly, he was showing me I could do the same.

I needed no more encouragement than that. Taking a short breath, I bid my host a silent farewell and popped up to the surface. The porpoise folk were all over me—swimming about and churning the water to foam. Each wanted to touch this exotic creature who lived on the land, and I was nearly drowned in overtures of friendship.

Seeing them there in great number, bobbing about in the water, it suddenly occurred to me where I had seen such a sight before. Surely these were the very same creatures who had appeared so many nights off the bow of the *Ahzir*, just before our encounter with the sea-thing! They could be no other!

The big male who had been with me from the beginning seemed to guess my thoughts, and I got another surprise on top of the first. Paddling up to me, he smiled and spoke in perfectly understandable Rhemian: "The Por'ai welcome you, Aldair. We have a great deal to tell one another."

Twenty-three

His name was Rah'neem, and his mate was called Cath'-
muur. I had imagined they were nobles of some sort, leaders
of their people, but this was not so at all. Indeed, I soon
learned that *no* one rules among the Por'ai, or wishes to do
so, for they believe it is wrong to set one being above another.
Incredible as it may seem, it is a system that appears to work
quite well for them.

"When you speak to us," Rah'neem said simply, "you speak
to us all." Only later did I come to understand the awesome
truth behind his words.

The Por'ai are a most kind and considerate people. They
were deeply concerned for my comfort, and did all they could
to keep me warm, dry and well fed in the cavern beneath
their city. I was given a heavy blanket of woven seaplants to
ward off the chill of my journey. There was bread of some
sort that tasted only slightly fishy, and a sweet-tasting broth
that spread a soothing warmth through my bones. I had quarters of my own, a small alcove off the main cavern, though I
spent little time there save for sleeping.

Rah'neem apologized profusely for taking me by surprise
beneath the *Ahzir*, and bringing me to the city against my will.
I came to learn that this act was indeed most painful for them
both, for the Por'ai are nearly incapable of forcing their wishes
on another.

It was Cath'muur who suggested I let my friends know immediately that I had come to no harm. When I told her I
would be delighted to do this, if it was possible, she quickly
came up with an answer. I had to laugh at her solution to this
problem, for she readily produced an empty clay jar that had
been tossed overboard from the *Ahzir* itself! In fact, the
container still smelled faintly of sour wine.

Cath'muur produced a rather brittle piece of dry seaplant,

the inky substance from the shell of some creature, and a pliant root to write with. I scrawled a short message which read: "Don't worry, I am alive and well and among friends. Aldair." This missive was placed in the jar, sealed, and bobbed to the surface in plain sight of my companions. Later, I was assured it had been retrieved.

There is much to tell about my stay among the Por'ai. To recount all that I learned from these people would require a weighty volume in itself. Thus, I have done my best to record those portions of our talks which were of the greatest import and interest.

I was most surprised to learn that while to now we knew nothing about the Por'ai, they knew a great deal about us. Once, when I asked Rah'neem about this, he deftly set the question aside.

"To understand the ways of the Por'ai, you must first know what we are," he explained. "We are not the same as other races, Aldair. You are born of the land, and we are born of the sea—but there is much more between us than that. I must tell you that we are an old race, much older than any other on Earth, for we were the first of the New People."

"The—New People?" At his words, a chill started at the base of my spine. I studied him carefully, trying to read some meaning in his features.

He smiled, turning slowly in the water. "Come, Aldair— you know very well what I am saying. We are both of the New People, you and I, as are all intelligent beings in the world. The Por'ai, however, were the *first* of Man's creations."

I let out a breath. "You *do* know, then!"

"Does that greatly surprise you?"

In a way, I suppose I was not surprised at all, but I could find no words at the moment, for my head was full of wonder. Here, then, in this great city beneath the sea, was a race that must surely know the secrets of Man! "The first of Man's creations. . . ." I hardly knew I spoke the words aloud.

"We are indeed," he said, and a note of sadness touched his voice. "It is not a pretty tale, Aldair, but it is one you must hear if you would understand the Por'ai, and why we are what we are."

Thus, Rah'neem began the long story of the Por'ai and their

relationship with Man. He told how Man had held a special love for the porpoise folk since he first began to sail the seas. Even then, in ancient times, he believed the porpoise had powers of intelligence far greater than the other animals about him. Later, when his knowledge grew, he found a way to understand the sounds of the porpoise, and make his own words understood as well. It was a crude form of communication, but it was a beginning.

"Later still," Rah'neem explained, "when Man gained the power to change the shape of life itself, the porpoise was the first creature he turned to. Indeed, it was his interest in our ancestors that *sparked* this desire to bring real intelligence to the animals of the Earth."

"But *why?*" I interrupted, suddenly angry at all this. "How could he do such a thing, Rah'neem! I can't say I'm sorry I am what I am—still, ever since I learned that I was a—a *made* thing, I have tried to imagine what kind of being would *dare* to create another. Man had no right to take life in his hands and play with it like a toy. *It was not his to change!*"

For some reason, both Rah'neem and Cath'muur seemed visibly shaken by my words. They looked at one another for a long moment, saying nothing. Finally, it was Cath'muur who spoke. "You do not understand Man as the Por'ai do," she said. "He was neither god nor demon, Aldair, but a little of both. Like his creations, he was capable of the most noble deeds—or the lowest acts of degradation."

"The Men who gave true intelligence to our people were good men," said Rah'neem. "They had a dream, and whether they were right or wrong, it was a great and awesome dream indeed—to give the power of reason to every beast on Earth. To pass along that most precious of gifts!"

"The way you put it," I said darkly, "it sounds like a noble act, for certain. I just can't quite picture Man the great benefactor, Rah'neem."

The Por'ai shook his head. "What happened was never *meant* to happen. The power to change life was taken from the Men who would have used it wisely, Aldair. After the Por'ai were created, it was never used again to make companions for Men. Instead, those who stole the gift made servants, toys—and monsters. It was then that the Por'ai turned away from Man, and fled to the depths of the sea. And it was well we did, for the Men who had taken the power now

hated and feared the Por'ai. We were the only other race on
Earth who shared their intelligence, and for this they decided
we must die. For centuries they sought us out, and slaughtered
us by the millions. They sent great and terrible weapons
against us. They poisoned the seas, and created hunter-crea-
tures to find and destroy our cities. If we had not been born
to the depths and known its secrets well, we could not have
survived their wrath."

"We knew what Man was doing to himself," said Cath'-
muur, "and this knowledge brought sadness to the Por'ai. For
we of all creatures knew what he could be, and how far he
had fallen. Still, there was little we could do but save ourselves. He had tasted the wine of the gods—he was more than
Man, now, and something less."

Again, Rah'neem took up the story. "Finally, in the last
days of his madness, he committed the greatest sin of all. He
was no longer capable of the noble act of creation, Aldair.
At the end, he could do no more than mock his own sad folly.
This, in essence, is what he did. He created parodies of himself, and gave them life—"

"—and bound them to the chains of his own damnable
history!" I finished, trying hard to keep the anger from my
words. "And all this time your people knew, Rah'neem. From
the very beginning!"

Rah'neem held up a hand. "Yes, we knew, Aldair. We knew
the lie you lived from the moment of your creation. And before you ask the question I am sure is in your mind, ask this
one of yourself: what could the Por'ai have done, truly? For
several thousand years you were little more than savages, like
every race in its infancy. You lived your lives in the shadow
of fear and superstition, as Man intended."

"It has been some time since we huddled in caves and threw
rocks at one another!"

"True," he said, with a calmness in his voice that was more
than a little irritating. "But now that your races have grown,
now that the people of the world are more—enlightened, how
goes your quest, my friend? How much wiser are the folk of
all lands?" His dark intelligent eyes bore steadily into mine.
"Only a handful of beings name you brother and companion,
Aldair. You know yourself the rest would brand your secret
madness—if they'd care to listen at all!"

Later, when I took a moment to recall this conversation, I had to admit that he was right, of course—but this did little to cool the anger and resentment that burned within me. Perhaps I had no right to blame the Por'ai. I knew myself the danger of bringing "truth" to the world—the Good Fathers of Rhemia had taught me *that*. In Silium, I saw quite clearly that truth was often your own fine head on a pole above the gates of the city. Later, in far Niciea, the priests of Chaarduz gave me further instructions in this matter: to effectively bury a truth they wished suppressed, these worthies simply burned an empire to the ground around it.

Still, pain and anger ever colors reason, and I could not forget that the ancestors of the Por'ai had *been* there at the beginning. No doubt, as Rah'neem insisted, they were helpless to prevent the treachery of Man, being somewhat busy saving themselves. I understood this. I even believed it. But I could not bring myself to accept it. One cannot suffer ignorance, without resenting those who have not.

My two Por'ai friends were well aware of these feelings— and, as I came to learn, they had a ready answer for moments of conflict, and displays of emotion. They simply turned their powerful tails on end and swam away.

Sometimes, we spoke of other things besides the perfidy of Man, and I had occasion to learn a little about the Por'ai and their ways. Rah'neem and Cath'muur taught me how to make the proper shrill whistles that would bring the luminous sea-creatures to me whenever I wished. Soon, to my delight, I could guide them nearly any way I wanted, and I spent many long hours designing bright clusters of light in a dazzling array of colors.

I learned that there were many caverns like my own about the city, and that the air within them was constantly replenished by seaplants growing just below. As the Por'ai are mammals rather than fish, they must breathe fresh air the same as creatures on the land. With this marvelous system of air chambers at their call, they have no need to return continually to the surface.

"Still, no one stays below for very long," Cath'muur explained. "The Por'ai love the sun as well as the depths. We are creatures of two worlds, and we cannot be happy without a little of both."

Cath'muur's words bring up an interesting fact about the Por'ai. Being happy, I learned, was evidently the chief occupation of these people. Since they did not govern one another, they had no need for clerks or administrators. They did not war among themselves, so there were no great armies about. Farmers and traders were unnecessary, as everything one needed was either swimming about, or resting on the ocean floor.

Neither Cath'muur nor Rah'neem actually told me these things. For the most part, I guessed the truth about the Por'ai for myself. Admittedly, there was a great deal I did *not* learn, until the very end of my visit, but one can often learn a great deal from what *isn't* discussed in his presence. For instance, when I asked Rah'neem about the occupations of the Por'ai, or said I would like to see more of the city and those who lived there, he quickly changed the subject. This was most irritating, but it was also quite enlightening. What, I wondered, did these friendly people have to hide? Why was I kept alone, away from the rest of the city? I was a well pampered guest and could ask for no better treatment. But in truth, I had all the freedom of a bug stuck under a jar.

When I became overly curious about some forbidden topic, the Por'ai invariably turned the conversation back to me. They were most interested in stories about the land—what it was like, and what people did there. While they had observed us for many centuries, there was much they didn't know. This was quite understandable, as I imagine it would be most difficult to study several civilizations from just off shore.

Rah'neem was especially anxious to hear about my quest for the secrets of Man, and I was more than willing to oblige him. While I had learned a great deal about the past on Albion, and in other parts of the world, there was much I could only guess. Through Rah'neem, and his knowledge of Por'ai lore, I was able to fill in many gaps in the story. I learned how the races of Man had warred among themselves, using made-things and iron men to fight their battles. I learned how the last, most terrible war of all had nearly stripped the Earth and left it bare.

"Finally," said Rah'neem, recounting this tale, "no more than a handful of Men were left, scattered about the broken face of the Earth. Only the strongest, deepest Keeps survived, and there were thirty-three of these in all." The Por'ai paused, shaking his head. "If you have guessed the nature of Man, Aldair, you will not be surprised to learn that the survivors of this war were not content with their work. Who could call himself victor, while there were thirty-two other strongholds to challenge his might? Such was their madness that not one among them could bear the existence of the other.

"The final war of Man lasted thirty-three years, or so the legend says—though I'd guess there is some ancient reason why the two numbers match. At any rate, when it was over and done only a single Keep remained on the face of the Earth."

"And that would be Albion Isle," I said.

Rah'neem nodded. "Albion, of course."

"And having no further members of his own race to corrupt, he created the New People, and set them to living the whole damned tale all over again!"

"This is so," said Rah'neem. "Your race, and the others, were his successes, Aldair. You have seen some of his failures—the Men-beasts in Merrkia, the thing that attacked your ship off the Great River—"

"What!" I sat up straight at that, for he had pointedly ignored my questions on this subject before. "*That* thing was a creature of Man?"

"It was," said Rah'neem. "It is called the *Briah'nn-Ruus* among the Por'ai—the devourer of all things. Once, the place it lived was Man's dumping ground of life. The things he left there should have died, but they did not. They clung together, grew, and became one great and terrible creature. It had neither mind nor purpose—only hunger."

"And it is truly gone now?"

"It is."

"And the flying thing," I put in quickly, "the craft that came to save us."

Rah'neem looked surprised, as if he'd forgotten for the moment this second strange phenomenon had a great deal to do with the first. It was a subject he had studiously avoided more than once.

"You—have asked me this before," he said coolly. "I will tell you again I know nothing about it, Aldair."

I found his eyes and held them. "I think perhaps you do,

Rah'neem." He stared at me, clearly bewildered, for I had never challenged him before. For the smallest part of a second I thought he would stand his ground and face me. Then, his Por'ai heritage won out, and with a great shower of water he disappeared beneath my pool. I must admit, these people have devised a most effective means of ending a conversation.

I come now to the end of my story of the Por'ai. As I mentioned in the beginning, I have not attempted to record every word of these talks, or to place conversations in the order in which they occurred. In many instances, I have combined two or more meetings for the stake of convenience.

Our last conversation is the exception to the rule, and I have tried to set it down exactly as it happened. There is good reason for this: the words that passed between us had a profound bearing on my future, and the future of my companions. Indeed, in the light of what came after, it would be safe to say there was scarcely a soul alive who was not affected by that moment.

As I had no way to measure the hours, it is hard to say how long I slept before I heard Rah'neen call my name. In truth, it seemed as if he had left me only moments before. I found him, as always, making small circles in the center of my pool. Cath'muur was not with him.

"I hope I have not disturbed your rest," he said. "It is important that we talk again, Aldair."

"You are welcome, as ever," I told him, saying the few words I had learned in the near impossible tongue of the Por'ai. Ordinarily, this seemed to please Rah'neem. Now, however, he was hesitant, distracted—not overly anxious to meet my eye.

"I must tell you," he said abruptly, "that it is time for you to leave the Por'ai."

I think I had been expecting this. "Rah'neem," I said carefully, "it is always good to rejoin old friends—but it is sad to part with new ones."

Rah'neem nodded vaguely, scarcely hearing my words. "We have not always been truthful with you, Aldair. I think you know this. There are questions we have not answered. Subjects we have refused to discuss. There are reasons for this. I would have you understand that."

"I never wished to pry into things that did not concern me," I told him. "I have asked questions because I am interested in the Por'ai, and because they possess knowledge of great importance."

Rah'neem nodded impatiently. "We know this, Aldair. As I said, there are reasons. It is not easy for the Por'ai to lie—to ourselves, or to any other. It is a most—painful thing for our people."

"I have learned there is much that is painful for the Por'ai," I said. "It may be that the truth hurts less than a lie, but I think there is a great deal more to it than that. It is not easy for you to talk to me at *all*, is it, Rah'neem?"

He looked up, startled. "You have guessed more than we imagined," he said soberly. "If this is so, it will be easier for me to say what I have to say." Finally, he faced me squarely. "You have asked more than once why we brought you here, Aldair. No doubt, you have wondered why the Por'ai chose this moment to show themselves to the world, when we have hidden these many years from the landfolk. The answer is simple. We *had* to make our presence known. You left us no choice in the matter."

"You meaning *who?*" I asked, for his words puzzled me greatly. "Rah'neem—"

"Wait, Aldair. Listen, and you will understand. I told you once that we are not the same as other races—that there are great differences between us. You have guessed a part of that difference, but you can scarce imagine the rest. You were right in what you said—it *is* painful to talk to you. We take joy in your being, and in the being of all creatures. *But we cannot tolerate your presence!*"

"But, why, Rah'neem? Are we really so different? It seems to me we have much in common—"

Rah'neem laughed ruefully. "You still do not see, do you? Why do you think we flee when you show anger, Aldair? And have you not wondered why you have met no more than *two* of the Por'ai, out of the millions in our city?"

"I know you are—sensitive to anger," I said, "and in truth I thought it somewhat strange that I was kept here alone—"

"You were kept here alone," he said plainly, "so you could cause no harm to the others."

"Harm? *What* harm, Rah'neem!"

"The harm you cause by *being*. By thinking, feeling, having life. For this is both our strength and our weakness, Aldair. It is the real reason Man sought so hard to destroy us. It is not a sense he gave us, but it is there, and always has been." His dark eyes fastened on mine. "We share the thoughts of others, Aldair. Not all, but those strong enough to touch us. Anger, hate, fear—and love, of course. It is a strange and terrible gift. It brings pain—and joy. You felt that joy yourself, when we soothed your fears on the journey here."

"Do you—" I could hardly believe what I was hearing. Still, there was no other answer to the things I had experienced among the Por'ai. *Do you know what I am thinking? Is this true, Rah'neem?* I did not say the words aloud. Suddenly, his own came back to me clearly, as if he were speaking: *It is true, Aldair. There are no more lies between us.*

I was near startled out of my wits at this. It is a most peculiar thing to hear words in your head!

Rah'neem smiled. "You see? You did not guess everything."

"No," I admitted, "I did not. It's a thing I would never have dreamed. It answers much—"

"—But not all," he finished.

"No. Certainly not all. It does not tell me *why* I was brought here. You have yet to answer that."

Rah'neem nodded. "It was not an easy thing to do, Aldair. The thoughts of others are more painful than you can imagine. We watched you, and followed your ship for some time, you know. We were curious, particularly when we learned what you were about. But we could not bring ourselves to approach you—we could not even warn you of the *Briah'nn-Ruus*, even though we knew it was in your path."

"Did you *need* to warn us, Rah'neem?" The thought was suddenly there. Whether it was mine or his I could not say. "I think you *knew* that something would save us from disaster—that we would not be swallowed by the sea-thing. I think the Por'ai do more than read the thoughts of others— they know events to come as well!"

Rah'neem studied me a moment. "Yes, we knew. Or thought we knew. The future is very much like a dream, Aldair, and dreams do not always reflect the truth of the world. The Por'ai themselves do not fully understand this, and I would say no more about it."

"You *know* about that craft," I insisted, "the one that bears a likeness of the *Ahzir!*"

"Aldair," he said calmly, "put aside all thoughts of mysterious craft for the moment, and hear what I have to say. It is most important that you understand *why* the Por'ai risked a great deal to bring you here."

"You've already told me *I* was the reason, though I can't see how this could be."

"It can *be,*" he said bluntly, "because we read your thoughts aboard the *Ahzir* and learned what you were about—that you were determined to toss everything aside, to abandon the quest that others had set before you. Nothing less than this could have made us show ourselves!"

I stared at him, anger fast overtaking my surprise and disbelief. "You *too?*" I blurted out. "Creator's Eyes, another bedamned seer to guide me off to nowhere!"

He turned away from my wrath, but stood his ground. "You must not stop now, Aldair—*whatever the cost.*"

"Why," I said, tasting the bitterness of my words, "so I can lose *another* shipload of friends?"

"Because I am telling you what the Por'ai have known for a thousand years before your race was born. That Albion was *not* the only stronghold to survive the last war of Man. There was another, a thirty-fourth, and the Men who built it called it Amazon Keep. It is still there, Aldair, and it is worth all you have to give to find it. . . ."

Twenty-four

———◆———◆———

Sailing the great Amazon is not the same as sailing some ordinary river. Indeed, it is so vast and awesome one imagines he is adrift on a broad and muddy sea. Our ancient chart showed that it narrowed eventually, but this seemed hard to believe at the time. The *Ahzir* sailed many leagues before the shore became more than a dim gray smudge on either side.

A river of such size has its own peculiar hazards. Often, trees near as big as the ship itself came floating down to meet us—some so enormous their ragged branches towered above the mast. Needless to say, these encounters did little to comfort Signar-Haldring. Such obstacles could be avoided by day, but night was something else again. We had no intention of putting in to shore—on the other hand, we could not risk being crushed after dark by some gigantic bit of garbage.

We solved this dilemma by turning it to our favor. The trees that swept downriver often became entangled with others, until the mass of the whole anchored them firmly to the bottom. Soil, branches and other debris collected there and eventually formed large islands in midstream. Plants and small trees quickly flourished, and creatures of every kind took up residence. I would not have set foot on one of these verminous mounds for all the gold in Rhemia, but they made excellent protective harbors for the night.

On our fifth day upriver, we took refuge behind a particularly noisome isle which I am certain sheltered every insect and varmint on the Amazon. The moment we dropped anchor, great clouds of bugs descended upon us. Small, invisible creatures scurried about and plopped into the water. Corysia, standing beside me, shuddered as a white-bellied snake as thick as my waist slithered through the foliage.

"I wonder if that child's mother knows it's out," I said idly.

Corysia made a face. "If that *child's* got a mother, I don't care to see it. Have you ever imagined a place so thick with *life*, Aldair? Everywhere you look something's moving, crawling about."

"I think *teeming jungle* is the phrase you're searching for."

"I had something worse in mind," she nodded, "but that'll do. When we stopped last night I was up here alone awhile. You were back with Signar and Thareesh somewhere. I watched this one single plant a long time, only I thought it was a snake or something because it kept moving. Finally, I realized it *was* a plant. I was watching it *grow*, Aldair. I couldn't believe it, but that's what it was doing."

"It's a wonderful place for a cruise," I said. "Heat, bugs, dirty water—the Amazon's got everything."

"It has what we're searching for," she said. I don't think she meant for the words to come out that way. There was no anger or admonition in her voice, but there was something. When I turned to face her I knew I was right, for she quickly looked away.

"Come on, Corysia. Say what's on your mind. There is no need for subtleties between us."

For a long moment she said nothing. Then: "I—guess I am more concerned with what is on *your* mind, Aldair. I know you well, love, and I know you are not content with this."

"This what?"

"This venture, of course. You know very well what I am talking about. You are committed, but your heart is not in it. I know this, and so do the others."

"I have made no great secret of my feelings," I reminded her.

"No, *that* you have not."

I looked up at her, somewhat surprised. If there had been no anger before, it was clearly there now. "Just how do you imagine I should *be*, Corysia? I changed my decision—not my thinking. I am still not enthusiastic about leading my friends to slaughter."

She shook her head fiercely. "If you really believed that, Aldair, you would never have changed your mind!"

"I did *not* change my mind, remember? I changed my vote, so to speak. It is not the same thing."

"You are convinced we are sailing into another disaster."

I laughed, tasting the bitterness of my words. "Not *con-*

vinced, Corysia. And you're right. Damn me, if I was convinced of such a thing, we wouldn't be here! Still, what kind of fool would I be if I did not remember what has gone before? Is there any need to list those follies again? I will, if you like, though I think you know them well."

She turned away for a long moment, staring at the darkening water. "You said you believed the Por'ai."

"I did, and I do. If I did not, we would not be sailing up the Amazon. Not under my command, for sure. The Por'ai are incapable of lying, Corysia. I am near certain of that."

"Then you believe there is a thirty-fourth Keep somewhere ahead of us."

"*They* do. The Por'ai. And it will not surprise me if they are right." I gripped her shoulders so hard she winced under my touch. "Corysia, *look* at me, will you? Isn't it enough that I have done what I have done? Must I set my face in a lie as well? I cannot see how this would be of value to any of us!"

She placed her hands on mine and coolly took them from her shoulders. "Then you do not know your companions as well as you might," she said stiffly, "nor your lover either, it seems. Every person aboard the *Ahzir* looks to you to set his courage. Don't you know that, Aldair? It is not enough that you have changed your mind. If you don't *believe*, then they don't believe, either. Maybe there *is* some danger they'll need to face on the morrow, or the day after that. They'll face it well, as you know—but not if you take the heart out of them, Aldair. Do that, and you will surely have their blood on your hands!"

In truth, I could not deny the wisdom of her words. In the light of what came to pass, I might have done well to don a false face and keep a great many of my feelings to myself—on this and other matters. Though I am not at all certain it would have made much difference in the end. . . .

Aside from floating trees, there appeared to be little danger in sailing the great river. The most hazardous part of our journey was well behind us, as far as the *Ahzir* was concerned. The Por'ai had guided us safely past the broad delta with its treacherous currents and sandbars, and promised to meet us there on the way back. Still, Signar-Haldring planted numerous poles and flags to mark the way, and carefully noted our course on his personal charts.

"Just in case," he growled meaningfully, and I knew very well what he had in mind. More than once, the Vikonen had pointed out that while the Por'ai were just as fine a folk as you could ask for, they *had* left us at the delta, making it clear as day they didn't intend to go farther. I explained again that these were a most unusual people, and extremely shy of other races—information which did nothing to dissuade him. Facts only get in the way when a Vikonen has made up his mind. In this respect, they are nearly as bad as the Stygianns.

"I ain't asking them to bunk in with me," he said darkly, "but it wouldn't hurt none to swim a little ways upriver and kinda scout things out, now would it?"

I had no answer to this, other than the facts at hand. And though I said nothing to Signar, the desirability of such an arrangement had occurred to me as well. None of us had forgotten the disaster of Merrkia.

I did not intend to give the impression that there were no hazards to our journey. Danger was all around, if you cared to look for it. The jungle on either side was alive with animals and serpents of every sort, and the river itself was quite deadly. Just how deadly we did not imagine until we discovered by accident what lurked beneath the waters.

Rhalgorn, who despised the taste of fish, took an almost childish joy in catching them. On our ninth day upriver, he decided to try his luck, swearing by every oath imaginable that he could see enormous fish beneath the muddy waters. From somewhere in his cache he produced half a hare so rancid even a Stygiann wouldn't eat it. Wrapping a whole tangle of hooks about this specimen, he dropped it over the side on the end of his line. In less than three seconds, the water was alive with ravenous creatures thrashing around his bait. Before he could pull it up again, the poor hare was a bundle of bones, picked clean and white as you please.

Rhalgorn stared at the thing a moment, then dropped bait, pole and line over the side and stalked below decks.

Later, we caught several of these creatures in a net and got a chance to look them over. They are nearly all jaw, and their teeth are as sharp as a fine Niciean blade.

"I hope there is no more trouble with the rudder," I told

Signar. "I am not overly anxious to go for a swim, and I don't expect Barthius or Stumbaucius will go in my place."

Signar pretended to listen, but the sly grin across his muzzle told me his mind was on other matters. I learned what this was about a few days later, as did Rhalgorn, who found one of these small monsters in his bedding. From his howl, it was clear they are fearsome things to sleep with, even when they are dead.

There is little more to tell about our journey upriver. One day easily describes another. There were hidden dangers and very visible discomforts. Insects. Heat. Rain. Aches and fevers. Finally, on the dawn of our fifteenth day a'sail, we came upon Amazon Keep. It was no more dramatic than that. We simply rounded a bend in the river and it was there —or at least its beginnings.

Flush along the shore was a great wall of Man-stone, twice as high as the mast. It was cracked and grown over with foliage, but very much intact. Sailing closer, we could see it stretched near half a league along the river.

"Don't look too easy to get *into*," growled Signar.

"There'll be a way," I told him.

"And how d'you figure that?"

Before I could answer, Rhalgorn stabbed a finger at the wall. "Aldair's right," he said darkly, "if you poor fellows had half the eyes of a Stygiann, you'd see the doorkeep himself is on hand to greet us!"

I looked, but saw nothing. Signar glared at Rhalgorn, then grabbed his spyglass and turned it to the wall. Immediately, the hackles on his back went stiff with anger. "Creator's Eyes, I don't believe what I'm seein', but there it is, sure as sin. It's Man himself, Aldair—all dressed up in shiny armor, just as big as you please!"

Twenty-five

—◦◦•◦◦—

I had no more than a second or so to view this bizarre creature for himself. He stood unmoving atop the high battlement, the sun turning his gaunt, armored frame to silver. His helm was firmly fixed and I could not make out his features. Still, I clearly felt the cold, razor glare of his eyes upon me. He studied us another long moment, then turned away, a splinter of light against the morning.

Signar wasted no time bringing us sharply about, out of the shadow of the wall. We could yet be in danger, but it was something of a comfort to face that awesome expanse of stone from a distance. A quick glance told me every warrior was at his station, weapon and shield at the ready. They did not speak to one another, or look aside from the shore, and I am certain every being aboard shared a single thought at that moment: *It is Man! Man is here. . . !*

We were prepared to find his Keep, for we had walked in the dust of his boots more than once. But to meet the great foe himself, standing like a lord atop his mighty wall. . . .

I felt the Vikonen move silently up beside me, Thareesh in his shadow. Both, I noted, lightly clasped the hilts of their blades, though I am certain neither was aware of this.

"Well, what do we do now," asked Signar, "just sit here starin' at stone?"

"It is his move," I said, "we will wait and see what he does."

The Vikonen made a noise. "Knowin' what kindly folk they are, I can guess what *that'd* be!"

"This thought has crossed my mind, as well," hissed Thareesh.

"And mine," I told them. "If he is indeed Man, and I cannot imagine who else he would be in this place, it is

139

useless to turn away now. If just one of his ancient weapons
remains intact—"

"Ah, there!" Thareesh pointed. Following his gaze to shore
we saw a shadow crease the great wall, only a meter above the
river. The shadow grew to a portal, then suddenly filled with
light.

"Holy Creator," muttered Signar.

My mouth went dry at the sight, though I have seen the
lights of Man below Albion. They neither waver nor dim,
but burn with a cold and steady glow, like tiny captive suns.
It is an awesome thing to see, and takes some getting used to.

"There is our friend again," said Thareesh. Indeed, it was
the same creature, or one much like it. He strode into the
light, stopping close to the edge of his portal. Then, with no
more than a glance our way, he raised his hand and clearly
gestured us to him.

Beside me, Thareesh took a breath and held it.

"Damn me," growled Signar, "what kind of fools does he
take us for?"

"He's judged us right enough," I said.

The Vikonen started to protest, but Thareesh stopped him.
"What else would you have us do—turn and sail away again?"

"I'd use the sense the Creator gave me, for one thing!
There's gotta be a better way than just—marchin' right in
where he wants us."

"And what would that be?"

Signar bit his jaw and scowled at the Niciean. "I'm thinkin'
on it. Whatever it is, *this* ain't it, for certain." He looked to
me for encouragement, and found none. Knowing me as well
as any creature knows another, he decided it was useless to
say more. "I'll get a longboat ready," he muttered darkly, "unless you're figurin' on swimming."

"The small boat'll do," I called after him. "There'll only be
myself and another."

"—And that would be me," said Thareesh, stepping quickly
to my side.

Rhalgorn studied us carefully a moment, then honored us
with a wry Stygiann frown. "Meaning no offense to you
mighty warriors, but it might be you'll need a little extra
muscle over there, if you intend to conquer the entire Keep
of Man."

I laughed and clasped him on the shoulder. "Your point is

well taken, old friend—but I'll give you another in its place. If there's danger there, a thousand Stygianns will serve us no better than one. This is a race with little respect for swords and longbows."

"Perhaps," Rhalgorn said stiffly. "Though it is hard to imagine anything born to Earth that would be foolish enough to turn its back on a Stygiann blade."

I said nothing to Corysia, for we have been together too long to need words between us. I saw her once from the longboat, looking small and far away. A glance passed from her eyes to mine, and I turned quickly back to my oars.

"No doubt good Rhalgorn is right," said Thareesh. "This is probably a very foolish venture, Aldair."

"There is little question of that," I agreed. "What is the thing doing, Thareesh? Is it still where it was?"

The Nicean squinted past my shoulder and gave a shrug. "It is doing nothing more than before, and no others have joined it. I would swear, Aldair, the creature has not moved a hair since it first appeared!"

"It is a Man—I would not expect it to behave like any normal creature."

"No, I suppose not."

"Still, I agree that it is behaving in a peculiar manner."

"It is more than peculiar, Aldair. What do you think we should do?"

"I think we should row," I told him, "or rather I think *you* should. This is hard work in such heat, and my arms are near finished."

I turned about as he took the oars, surprised to find we were only a few meters from the great wall. The sun blazed down upon the broad expanse of Man-stone, and the heavy growth clinging to its sides. The eerie glow which lit the dark opening was near lost in the greater light from above. And there, sunfire dancing off his armor, was the foe I had sought so long. His face was hidden to me still, but in only moments I might glance upon it at last.

What then, I wondered—when creator met his creation? Had time changed the temper of this terrible race? Were the Men of Amazon Keep any different from those who had bent the course of history for their pleasures? If they were not,

Signar would prove wiser than us all, and we would meet a sorry end indeed.

Suddenly, the moment was upon us. Thareesh brought the longboat around and I reached out to secure a line and hold us against the shore. Another, stronger hand came down to grasp my own, and Thareesh and I stared up at a dark metal face and eyes as cold as stone.

"Welcome to Amazon Keep," he said, and the raw, toneless voice near chilled me to the bone. "Your vessel will be secure here. Follow me, please. . . ."

With that, the creature turned away abruptly and disappeared down the long dark corridor, leaving Thareesh and me to gaze dumbly at one another.

"By all the gods, Aldair!—"

"I know," I said, grabbing his arm and glancing quickly back at the *Ahzir*. "I saw, Thareesh, and you are right in what you're thinking. This is *not* a Man at all, but another of his creations—some marvelous machine made to serve him. I should have guessed when I saw the thing, for the Por'ai spoke of such creatures! I never imagined we'd—"

The Man-thing stopped, peering back with red-coal eyes. "You must follow," it said shortly. "You do not know the way."

"I'm not at all sure I *want* to know the way," whispered the Niciean.

Still, follow we did, hands tight about our weapons. Even when one is certain the odds are against him, the hilt of a good blade is most comforting to the touch.

Our guide was right enough in one respect—we would have been lost in minutes without him. Though I tried to recall each twist and turn through that rocky maze, I soon gave up, hopelessly confused. We were getting an entirely different picture of the great wall of Amazon Keep. It was, in truth, no wall at all, but a massive, near endless block of Man-stone. On either side were corridors leading to unknown places, dark halls, and iron doors shut tight against us. For some reason neither Thareesh nor I could fathom, the light in this place was sometimes bright as day, sometimes so dim we could hardly see our guide. At no time did we see a sign of any other creature. It was a most uncomfortable feeling, for we imagined beings watching us from the shadows at every turn.

"I don't like this," said Thareesh. "There is something very wrong about this place."

"You are quite right," I agreed, "but I fear it's a little late to start worrying. I suspect it has *been* too late since we first set foot here."

Ahead, the iron-thing made still another turn—down a stone-walled way that differed not a whit from any other. I was becoming more than a little weary at this business. The creature clearly knew what it was about, but this was no comfort whatever to us.

"Thareesh," I said finally, "are you as tired of being an ant in a burrow as I am?"

"Most assuredly," said the Nicean. "I do not for the life of me think I could find my way back from this place, but I would be willing to make a try."

"It would be a useless try, at best, but there is another answer to this. If, Man wants to see us, he can find us where we are. You," I called out, "come back here!"

The thing hesitated, then turned its featureless face upon us. "You must follow, sir. You do not know the way—"

"No," I said, "we do not *intend* to follow. Not unless you tell us this instant where we are going!"

"—And when we're going to get there," added Thareesh.

The thing stood perfectly still, and I could almost hear the shiny metal thoughts whirring through its head. "We are going to Central, sir," it said tonelessly, "if that is your wish. If it is not, I will be pleased to lead you to Quarters. It is another four minutes to Central. A little more to Quarters. I—"

"We do not wish to see this Central or Quarters or whatever," Thareesh interrupted. "Tell your masters Aldair and Thareesh of the *Ahzir al'Rhaz* are here—wherever *here* is."

The thing looked at Thareesh, then at me. "I do not know what you are, sir," it said finally, "but you are a speaking being, therefore you are a master. I do not see how I can tell you that you are here, for you must be aware of this already."

"We do not care much for riddles," I warned him, gripping the hilt of my blade. "Go, creature, and tell Man the beasts he made would face him now!"

"I cannot do that," it said simply.

"Look, you—!" Thareesh started for him. I held him back.

"I cannot, sir, because Man is not here. Perhaps he will return, but this I do not know."

Not here? Thareesh and I stared at one another.

"What do you mean he's not here," I asked, "how long has he been *gone?* Do you know that, at least?"

"I do, sir—or think I do. As near as I can tell, it has been one hundred three point four centuries. Or is it one hundred four point three? You will forgive me, sir. Every day I find it a little harder to remember such things. . . ."

Twenty-six

———— ✦ ————

There is much to tell about Amazon Keep and the wonders it contained—more than enough to fill a volume in itself. Thus, I will not attempt to catalog its marvels; I will only say that it is a Man-place, and all that that entails—strange devices, puzzling artifacts and the ever-present ghosts of those who made them.

It is an alien place, yet strangely familiar. Men, we have come to learn, were not all that different from ourselves. This is not overly surprising when you remember that we, the beasts of Man, were patterned in his image. Still, for every sight that seems familiar, a hundred new perplexities spring to light. Every day we pose far more questions than we answer.

Certainly, one puzzle stands above the rest: why did Man abandon this place? Where did he go? The Keep was built as a fortress, a stronghold. That much is clear. Yet, it is wholly intact, undamaged. There is not a sign that it was attacked by hostile forces. This, as my companions and I agree, is perhaps the secret of Amazon Keep—that it played no part in that last, terrible war which destroyed the thirty-three strongholds of Man. And if this is so, perhaps the Por'ai were right— perhaps it is true that all Men were not the same. Certainly, the world today is peopled by creatures both good and evil and every degree between. By stretching the imagination a bit, I can almost imagine that Men were as varied in nature as we. . . .

If Amazon Keep was a sanctuary for Man, It has served us equally well. In the twenty days or so we have been here, miraculous changes have occurred in us all. We have turned from a haggard, sickly lot to strong and healthy beings. It is hard to recognize familiar faces among the crew, for many were near death from wounds and fever when we arrived. For the first time since our venture began, I have heard laughter untempered by the shadow of danger.

As in all things, however, this new-found reprieve from adversity has its darker side as well. I have never seen a coin with less than two sides, and Amazon Keep is no exception. The truth is, a warrior cannot handle too much ale and easy living. He will complain loudly in the midst of battle if there are worms in his bread, or if his ale has gone sour. Yet, after a week or so of peace and prosperity, he misses these things. His ale is too sweet and his bread too fresh from the oven. Moreover, since he has no true enemy to fight as such times, he fights whoever he can find among his fellows. And, being warriors themselves, they are only too willing to help.

Thus, Signar again had his hands full. Hardly a day went by without one mighty battle or another. "You know what they was fightin' about this time?" he growled, stomping into my quarters where Rhalgorn and I were sharing a cask of wine.

"I imagine you will tell us soon enough," yawned the Stygiann.

Signar gave him a baleful look. "There's some folks has time for a cool drink now then, and others that has to watch over 'em—lest they get their throats cut some fine evening."

"What is it this time?" I asked, offering a cold mug in the bargain. The Vikonen downed it quickly, then wiped a furry arm across his jaw.

"Onions," he said darkly.

"Onions?"

"Onions. Two of 'em, to be exact. One feller counted seven in his soup, and *nine* in his mate's. Damn near tore the creature's ear off."

"That's not much to fight about. Two onions."

"Damn, Aldair—it don't *take* much anymore,"

"He's right in that," added Rhalgorn. "A lazy warrior is as mean as a bucket of boils. We learned the truth of this long ago in the forests of the Lauvectii. You do not find the Stygianns sitting about snarling at one another—they are out raiding the lands of their neighbors, where they belong. This is why we are known as a peaceful, easy-going race."

Signar and I ignored this, knowing it is next to useless to argue with Stygiann logic.

Refilling our cups all around, I asked the Vikonen: "Is

Barthius at the bottom of this? If there's mischief about, I'd not be surprised to find him in the middle of it."

"You'd be right as rain, Aldair. He's got a hand in it, all right, but he's playin' it mighty careful now, lettin' others do the *loud* talkin' while he keeps to his self. You taught him a good lesson at sea, and he ain't forgot it."

"What I have done, I fear, is make him more cunning and wary," I said. "He has not learned to avoid trouble, he's learned to avoid me!"

Signar nodded grimly, his agate eyes dark with an anger he found hard to suppress. He knew I was right, but there was little he could do about Barthius, short of cutting his throat and tossing him over the Keep. This, of course, was not our way, as the wily Barthius well knew. In truth, I should have set mercy aside and heeded the wisdom of my fathers. Since I was a child in the Eubirones, I have heard it said that an act of kindness seldom goes unpunished. We would do well to remember that such sayings are soon forgotten unless they hold great meaning. . . .

As I have mentioned more than once, there is a lifetime of mysteries to be unraveled in Amazon Keep. Each new find, each peculiar artifact, opens the door to further speculation. Yet, in many ways, the things we have *not* found tell us much about the beings who lived here. I have said the Keep was a sanctuary. I am near certain, now, it was that and nothing more—for I have seen little to suggest great and terrible weapons or the fearsome Eye of Man. There are machines and devices a'plenty, but they do not have the look of war and destruction about them. This was a place where Men came to avoid *other* Men. I most earnestly believe this is true. There are vast chambers for eating and sleeping—great, empty caverns still lit with cold clusters of light. It was a place to hide and wait—but wait for *what?* Did Men with reason still about them huddle in this fortress while the terrible war of the thirty-three Keeps ravaged the world outside? Perhaps. It seems likely an answer as any. But, like many answers, it poses a most intriguing question: The Keep is still intact, which means they survived that holocaust. And if this is so, where are they now? Both good Men and bad once walked the earth, yet neither are with us still. *"Find Amazon Keep,"* the Por'ai told me. *"It is worth all you have to give!"* I have found it. I am here. And though it is not the same as other havens of Man I have known, it is not altogether different, either. Like the others, it hides its secrets well.

If I'd had half the sense of a turnip, I would have been grateful for this small favor. For as it happened, secrets I could well do without would reveal themselves soon enough.

Twenty-seven

———•◦⊷————◦•———

If hindsight is truly the wisdom of fools, I have massed a great storehouse of knowledge in my time. It is easy to turn the pages of the past and place a finger on this hour, and that day, and sagely mutter yes, there indeed was a moment of note, a turning point of great importance. Such a time, I know now, was the thirty-third day of our stay in Amazon Keep.

There are many who attach dire meaning to that number, seeing it is the same as the number of Keeps that savaged one another in ages past. To my thinking, such business is nonsense. While there is truly magic and wonder in the world, for the most part things happen when they happen. Be that as it may, those who search for obscure secrets will ever find them. Among the Niceans it is said that if one inspects enough ant dung, he will eventually find a pile that spells his name. Thareesh says this is not a true Nicean saying at all, but I am certain that is where I heard it. . . .

A seasoned warrior needs no star to tell him the hour. Thus, though I could scarce read the heavens from the bowels of Amazon Keep, I knew at once the dawn was near upon us when Signar's great boots pounded down the hall, jerking me out of sleep. Blade in hand before my eyes were fully open, I leaped up to meet him, leaving a startled Corysia behind.

The Vikonen's big form filled the door. He gave me a quick, bleary look, noted my sword and shook his head. "You won't need that. There ain't nothin' needs sticking, near as I can tell."

"Near as you can tell?" I said, scrambling into my jacket, "what's that supposed to mean?"

Signar made no attempt to hide his impatience. "Just get yourselves up an' dressed and don't ask a bunch of questions. When you see what there is to see, you can tell *me* what it is."

"Signar—"

149

Before the word was out, he was gone, leaving Corysia and me to stare at one another.

We learned no more on the way, for he made a point of striding well ahead of us both. This irritated me no end, and concerned me as well—for it was much out of character for Signar-Haldring.

Outside, the morning was still a pale stain against the stars —light enough to keep from stumbling about, but too dark for much more. The heavy pall of heat that chokes this land set us gasping, and in an instant we were wet as the air itself. It is easy to forget such discomforts in Amazon Keep, for Man made his own weather there, and his great machines have kept it so through the ages.

Our path led out of the Keep and to the west. I could hear the river on my right, but could see nothing through the thick tangle of foliage. Ahead, Signar stopped, waited a moment, then plodded quickly along. The sky was changing from azure to pale lemon yellow, and as we turned past a stand of dark-boled trees the Vikonen was suddenly there again, blocking our way. Behind him, down the path, was a loose circle of warriors and crewmen.

"It's up there," he said, still not catching my eye. "One of the scouts from the ship was lookin' for game and—he come straight to me, an' well—"

"Damn it all," I said, making no effort to hide my anger, "I am getting tired of this business, Signar. Stop your infernal muttering and step aside!" Without waiting for an answer, I pulled Corysia past him and stomped down the path. Warriors spoke my name, and quickly opened a way.

I cannot say what I expected to find—certainly, it was not the sight that greeted me in the clearing. A third, or near half of the thing was buried in the earth. The rest was covered in a thick layer of vines and roots that laced and bound it round like a captured beast. Even so, it was impossible to hide its awesome size, for it loomed above us like a golden star come down to rest.

Dropping Corysia's hand, I took a step forward. Then another. Warriors muttered warning sounds behind me. I laid a hand upon its side, felt the cold metallic surface, slick as good glass. There was not a touch of rust upon it, not a single scar of blemish. For all the ages it had slept there, it held the luster of a new-minted coin.

For a moment, I let my fingers linger there in wonder. It was a most curious, pleasant thing to touch. Then, knowing what I must do, I turned aside and started quickly around the object's flanks. It had to be there, of course, and every warrior and seaman at my back was waiting for me to find it. Only a few meters to the right and there it was, bright and new as morning. A blazing emblem of the *Ahzir al'Rhaz*, sails full to the wind, bow cutting a blue-green sea. Turning, I faced the circle about me, letting my gaze touch every creature there.

"It's a fair likeness, for sure," I told them, "though the lines are some loose in the rigging, and the sea's a bit heavy for such a sail."

It caught them unaware. They stared, jaws agape, certain I'd lost my senses. Then, a burst of laughter touched the circle, and the spell was broken.

"If there's riggin' to fix," said a big Vikonen seasman, "you can bet some fine Niciean's off sleepin' in the sun!"

More laughter, and a shrill Niciean voice from the other side of the group: "Who can find a spare line on the *Ahzir*? Fat Vikonens are wearing 'em all for belts!"

The tight circle of anxious faces fell away; warriors and seamen alike milled easily about the clearing, calling friendly insults and mild obscenities to one another. A few even dared approach the golden craft itself.

A dark-furred Vikonen, the fellow who'd started the laughter, walked up beside me and boldly touched a finger to the thing. "I seen a lot of questions on this venture that ain't got answers," he said, shaking his head in wonder, "but this one beats 'em all, Master Aldair. How d'ye figure it got here, all buried and such—and out to sea as well?"

"And why's it got *our* ship on its hull I'd like to know!" put in another.

"That's three good questions," I said, "and they'll *stay* just that for now—'less someone else cares to give 'em answers. It came from somewhere—out of the past as near as I can fathom, since it's clearly sat right here since the time of Man. How a ball of metal flies at all is wonder enough—I'd not attempt to guess how it plies between the years."

"There's one way easy enough," said a voice somewhere behind me, "though I don't guess Master Aldair'd care to—" The voice stopped abruptly, the speaker suddenly aware his words had carried much farther than he'd intended.

The clearing went silent. Turning, I picked out the speaker with no trouble, for I already knew his name. He was Sha'diir, a Niciean, and one of Barthius' own. Signar had pointed him out to me more than once.

"You are wrong," I said quietly, catching him squarely in the eye. "Master Aldair would be most grateful for your answers. Let's hear them now, so all may share your wisdom."

Sha'diir seemed to pale beneath his scaly hide. Those who'd clustered about him backed hastily away, and he was suddenly quite alone. To his credit, he stood his ground—though I suppose there was little else he could do.

"I—spoke in haste," he said glumly, "my words were—"

"—Not meant to be heard by me," I finished. A few quick steps and I stood before him. "Be that as it may, we will hear them now, Sha'diir. You are a free creature and no slave. You do not have to skulk about and whisper behind your hand." I turned, taking in every face about me. "I would make this clear to you all. Every being here is entitled to say what he wishes. Those who have sailed with me from the beginning know this is so. They also know," I added, facing Sha'diir again, "that I will listen to any seaman or warrior who meets me eye to eye—and that I have little patience for those who talk behind my back. Now—say again, to me, Sha'diir— what you would not say before!"

Sha'diir's lidless eyes grew dark. "I said nothing. I—"

"Speak, damn you!"

The Niciean started. A shadow of fear crossed his face. "I—I merely—I said there were *ways* such a craft could come and go as it wished. I—" Desperation gave him courage and the words came blurting out. "This is true, and I will say it now if you have my life for it! It is *demons* who steer such a vessel as this—demons from Hell itself! And it is they who paint our ship upon its side, for they have marked us for their own, *and they'll have the souls of us all before they're done!*"

At the mention of demons, several warriors paled and made signs upon themselves.

"Demons, is it?" I laughed in Sha'diir's face. "By the Creator, you'd best thank those *demons* and wish them well, for they saved your worthless hide out there! Have you so quickly forgotten what nearly ate us whole in the mouth of the river? I, for one, have not. Have the rest of you?"

"No, no!" they shouted, shaking angry fists at the Niciean. "We remember all too well, Master Aldair!"

Sha'diir turned on them. "There are worse things than *dying*," he hissed savagely. "You fools, don't you see? Are you blind to what's happening here?" His arm shot out stiffly, pointing at me. "He's *one* of them! A demon himself! I have *seen* him drink the blood of a—"

My fist came up and hit him squarely. It was not a thing I meant to do, but I could not have stopped it for my life. I felt the bones snap in his face. Saw the blood curl down his jaw. Someone shouted behind me, but I could not hear the words. I looked down—saw pain and triumph in Sha'diir's eyes. Looked up, and saw the others about me. It was easy to read what was there. The master does not strike the servant. For the servant cannot strike back.

I had made a terrible mistake. And I would pay for it. . . .

Twenty-eight

There is little value in recounting one's sins. They are neither lessened nor enhanced by the telling. Still, there is some satisfaction in knowing you are boring your friends as well as yourself—I believe I performed this act in a most exemplary manner, using some four or five hours and a like number of wine casks in the process.

"Well spoken, indeed," Rhalgorn said finally. "I think we can all agree that you have endangered our lives, set the crew against us, put our lives in jeopardy, and generally made an ass of yourself."

I sat down my mug and looked at him. "Did I say all *that?*"

"That, and a great deal more," said Corysia. "All any of us care to hear, Aldair."

I came to my feet, taking in Corysia and all the others. "I don't see how you can make light of this matter. I committed a most grievous error in striking Sha'diir. I lost control of myself, and that is unforgivable. I violated—"

"—All the rules of command," Thareesh finished. "We know that. And now that you have flailed yourself sufficiently, old friend, we would do well to drop the subject."

"And get on to something more productive," added Corysia.

"Such as?" I wanted to know.

"Such as how we can best *deal* with the situation, Aldair. Will you please sit down? You are making me nervous pacing about. What's done is done and there's no taking it back. And frankly, though you are determined to heap dung upon yourself, I am convinced *something* would have happened anyway. If you had not given them an incident, they would have created one."

"Maybe. But I didn't have to hand it to them on a platter."

"Nevertheless, you did," she sighed. "All right?"

154

"The feller deserved what he got," growled Signar, "and then some. *That's* for certain."

"That is hardly the point, Signar, and you damn well know it!"

"Didn't say it was, did I?" The Vikonen smothered a grin under his fist. "It's true, though," he said to himself. "I'm fried if it ain't."

The days that followed were quiet and without incident. This, of course, gave me no peace whatever, for I was certain it meant Barthius and his malcontents were merely biding their time, setting more of the crew against us.

My companions did their best to mend the fences I had so foolishly broken. Thareesh was particularly valuable in this respect, for the bulk of our sailors were Nicjean, and these fellows held him in high regard. Niceans are fiercely loyal, and most of our crew had served as either sailors or warriors under my own friend and former master, Lord Tharrin, the Aghiir. They had not forgotten that Thareesh was one of their own, that he had nearly given his life in the service of their king. I like to think they held me in some esteem as well, for no other foreigner in the history of Niciea had become *rhadaz 'meh* of the Aghiir.

"They have not forgotten who you are," Thareesh assured me. "Most of them are shamed by Sha'diir's treachery, and will have nothing to do with either him or Barthius."

In turn, Signar let me know that the Vikonen warriors and sailors were loyal to the end—that they would grind Barthius and his fellows into the dirt at the first hint of rebellion.

"Clearly, then, we have nothing to fear," I told my companions. "There is one Stygiann among us—you, Rhalgorn, and your loyalty is unquestioned. There are four members of my own race in Amazon Keep—Corysia, Stumbaucius, Barthius, and myself. Corysia and I are not in the rebel camp, and I do not think Stumbaucius is either. The rest of our crew is comprised of Vikonen and Nicieans. Thareesh and Signar assure me they are all completely loyal, save Sha'diir. That leaves two dissenters—Sha'diir and Barthius." I shrugged, waving the matter aside. "Not much of a rebellion, is it?"

No one spoke about our table. Finally, Signar-Haldring scratched his jaw and shook his head. "For bein' as bad as it is, it sure sounds good. Only it ain't, an' we all know that."

"We do indeed," I agreed.

Rhalgorn grinned wryly and licked his muzzle. "The answer is clear enough. Rebels seldom admit they are rebelling. It would be foolish and unseemly to do so. If I wished to slit my masters' throats, I would first convince them it is safe to sleep in my bed."

"What about Stumbaucius?" asked Corysia.

"What about him?"

"He likes you, Aldair. And respects you as well. He has shown he is a friend."

I saw where she was going and shook my head. "He is all of those things. But first he is a soldier. If you'll recall, he would not betray Barthius, even in the beginning. He would not spy for me, and I would not ask him. On the other hand, if the rebels make their move, I am certain he would break that warrior's code of his and warn us."

"Not if they move, Aldair—*when*," said Rhalgorn. His blood-red eyes moved quickly about, touching us all. "And do not count on Stumbaucius, for he will not be there to warn us. Barthius is not so foolish as that. When he is ready, your fine Rhemian warrior will be the first to feel the blade."

Rhalgorn's words hit me like a breath of wintry air. He was right, of course, and I was both shamed and angered that this had not occurred to me before. I could think of little else that evening, and cannot for the life of me recall what we talked about.

By noon the next day several suggestions for quelling rebellion were laid at my door—none seemed overly useful, but I thanked the bearers for their thoughts. Signar suggested we disarm everyone, thereby assuring that whoever the rebels were, they would have no weapons. He was not too fond of this idea himself, for it was he who pointed out no less than seven reasons why it would do more harm than good. I will not even mention Rhalgorn's idea, for it was neither practical nor wholesome in nature.

I have said little about the discovery that sparked this problem, and gave strength to Barthius and his fellows. While I will not lessen my own role in that incident, I am convinced the golden craft itself played a part in fomenting dissent among my crew. Warriors and seamen are a superstitious lot at best—they might scoff at Sha'diir's "demons" by day, but when night's upon them in a strange land, it's a different cup of ale altogether. They hardly *need* a hint from Barthius to see devils of every shape and size prancing about.

And what could *I* give them, in place of cold and fearsome ghosties? The sound, "reasonable" answers I can imagine are more bizarre than any they could conjure up themselves! Where did the thing come from, how did it fly from one age to another to save us from the sea-thing? And, most chilling of all—*who crewed that vessel, and set the image of our ship upon it?*

This last, of course, brings some intriguing questions to the fore—questions I would just as soon not dwell upon. I do not like to think about those two occasions in my life when I met the specter of myself—once, at sea, and again on the fateful bridge over Rhemia. Still, it is a question I must ask: is this new mystery somehow akin to that? The golden craft itself is no specter, for I have touched it, and it is real. Yet, it bears my mark upon its hull—and *that* is real as well. Like the shades of myself that were, and then were not, this is a thing that cannot be—but is.

If that seer who sometimes guides my path can hear these words, I would tell him again that I am not cut out for this kind of work. I have my hands full dealing with *this* world and time, and I do not feel qualified to handle any others. . . .

We have a saying in the Eubirones that states fine wine and sour ale both look the same inside a dirty crock. Good Stumbaucius proves the truth of this, for I had judged him as he truly seemed to be—a loyal, steady and wholly unimaginative soldier, cast in the traditional Rhemian mold. Thus, I was both surprised and pleased with his interest in Amazon Keep. For near the beginning of our stay, I learned he was spending all his free time wandering about the vast network of chambers, sniffling into this corner and that, and even recording his treks on a very formidable looking chart. Naturally, I encouraged this, as his interests mirrored my own, and I soon relieved him of all other duties and put him in charge of mapping the entire Keep.

Stumbaucius, of course, was delighted. He attacked the project like an assault upon an enemy stronghold, and soon knew near as much about the place as the Men who built it.

Later, as the trouble with Barthius intensified, I was glad his work kept him apart from the others. As Rhalgorn had so pointedly reminded me, there was no love lost between those two. Thus, Stumbaucius became a familiar sight long the corridors of Amazon Keep—an intent, very industrious fellow with a Metal-Man ever tagging behind, its spidery arms full of dusty charts and papers.

I have said little about these Metal-Men, for there is indeed little to tell. That there was more than one about the place did not occur to us until two appeared together one day. I then learned there were seven in all—that each had been among us at one time or another, and we had never noticed the difference. They had names, assigned to them by Man, I suppose, though this seemed next to useless if we could not tell one from another. Stumbaucius eventually put an end to this problem by daubing each creature's name across its chest in bright red paint. Thus, one knew if he was speaking to Lis, Katho, Jon, Sib, Jer, or Dann—though it made no difference one way or the other, as each knew as much, or little, as the next.

Any hopes I had of learning the secrets of Man from these fellows were doomed to disappointment. They knew everything there was to know about Amazon Keep—except what *I* wanted to know. They could tell you where this series of thingamabobs should be stored, or where that carton of whatever could be found, and a thousand other bits of information. Fascinating data, if you enjoyed warehouse procedures several thousand years in the past.

I have said there were seven Metal-Men, and mentioned only six. The last was called Wall-drop, a name coined by Stumbaucius because the fellow had evidently dropped in its tracks by a wall one day. Now, it merely sat there gathering dust, looking intently out at nothing. If its wheels whirred about inside, I couldn't hear them, even if I put my ear to its head. Neither could I say whether it had been sitting there a month before our arrival, or a hundred centuries more. In truth, it hardly matters, for time moves slowly as summer shadow in Amazon Keep. . . .

Twenty-nine

———◆—◆—◆———

"I have something of great interest to show you, Master Aldair—great interest indeed!"

This, from the stern and sober Stumbaucius, caught my attention right well, for he is not the most excitable fellow I've met.

"Good," I said, "though I'd hope it's not *too* interesting, Stumbaucius—one more miracle of Man around here will do me in for certain."

His jaw went slack at that. For a moment, he looked totally bewildered. "Oh—it is nothing like that, sir—truly!"

"No," I told him gently, "I am sure it isn't. I am at my wit's end these days, old friend, and that is no fault of yours. Now—take a chair and tell me what you have."

He relaxed a bit, but stood where he was. Turning to the ever-present Metal-Man behind him, he found a thick roll of charts and flattened them out before me.

"You have seen this before, sir, but there's much more to it, now. See here—" He ran a finger over the paper, "—you'll recall, sir, there's nine levels in all in the Keep, an' each has a proper use—such as sleeping, eating, and storing things—though it's hard to tell where one leaves off an' the other begins, what with halls and passages of every sort twistin' this way and that. Now, here's the thing of it, Master Aldair. . . ." He tapped the chart at its very edge. "I've learned there's another level as well. A tenth, somewhat below the others."

I waited to see if there was more. "So? I am not overly surprised, for Man seemed near as fond of tunnels as a hare is."

Stumbaucius looked pained. "Your pardon, sir, but that's not the whole of it. I don't know the *use* of the place, an' I'm near certain the Metal-folk don't either."

"Did you expect them to?" I studied him a moment, wondering if the fellow had been spending too much time with metal creatures. They say even stones and radishes become quite interesting to talk to if there's nothing else about. Stumbaucius guessed my thoughts, for the color rose to his cheeks. "That's true and it isn't, sir." He frowned thoughtfully, scratching the bristles of his snout. "There's things they know an' things they don't. I'm more certain of that."

"—And things they know and don't *talk* about," I added.

Stumbaucius nodded, a bit reluctantly. "Right enough, sir, but that's somethin' else again. What I'm saying is they each kind of know what they're *supposed* to know—and not a lot more'n that. It's like—well, like they were built to do certain things, an' that's what was put in their heads."

"That's an interesting point. I'd say you're close to right."

"Yes, sir—and that's the thing, you see. This new level I'm talkin' about. Doesn't any of 'em know what it's *for*. And I'm near certain they don't *know*. I can't say why, I just am."

From the ring of his words, I knew he firmly believed this. "Well, what does the place appear to be, then? Can you make a guess, from the others you've seen?"

Stumbaucius looked blank. Then, he slapped the side of his head and gave a low moan. "Master Aldair, your pardon. Puttin' words together ain't the best thing I do, for certain. I didn't even tell you, did I? I got no idea about that level 'cause I've not been *in* it. It's locked up tight as a keg and there's no way through, near as I can see."

"Locked up, you say?" I studied this matter in a new light, for curiosity is a great fault among my people—one that frequently leads to shorter tails and snouts.

"Locked indeed, Master Aldair." He was pleased with himself now, and showed it. "I thought it'd be of interest to you, sir."

"Stumbaucius," I said darkly, "as I told you in the beginning, it had better not be *too* damned interesting. . . ."

Sure enough, it was just as the warrior had said. Down a narrow stair below the ninth level was another—or the start of one, at least. For the stairway ended abruptly against a high metal door set in solid stone.

"Well, what do you make of that?" I asked Rhalgorn. Stygianns are even nosier than the folk of Gaullia, though they do not care to admit it. Thus, since I saw no reason to tell Rhalgorn where we were going, he immediately invited himself along.

"That is clearly a door, all right," he said thoughtfully. "I would guess it leads to something *else*, too, on the other side."

"That is a marvelous observation," I told him. "I am grateful for your help."

Rhalgorn sniffed and looked away. "Say what you will, Aldair. Mocking the efforts of others will get you no closer to an answer."

"Is that what that was? An effort?"

"The beginnings of one. If you will use your one remaining ear to listen, you will doubtless hear the rest of it." Rhalgorn looked past Stumbaucius, to the Metal-Man behind him. "If you want answers," he said, pointing, "ask this pile of tin that walks like a person. *It* knows what's going on in this place, for certain!"

"Stumbaucius and I have discussed this earlier," I told him.

"We have, sir," said Stumbaucius.

"Ah, no doubt." Rhalgorn gave us a knowing smile. "But you have not discussed it with this tin thing."

"*I* have," put in Stumbaucius. "More times than I can tell you, sir. There's things they know they ain't saying, I'll grant you that. But I *know* this isn't one of 'em."

The Stygiann was not impressed. "Perhaps you are simply not phrasing the question properly. There is a right way and a wrong way to go about these things, you know." With that, he drew his heavy blade and raised it high over his head. "*You*," he snapped at the Metal-Man, "kindly open this door or I will loose that bucket from your shoulders!"

Stumbaucius looked appalled. The Metal-Man said nothing.

I tried to stop, but laughed aloud. "I fear this poor fellow is not familiar with the Stygiann path to reason."

Rhalgorn glared, "He had damn well better learn, then." He lowered his sword. Stumbaucius looked relieved, but Rhalgorn was not entirely finished. He stomped up to the Metal-Man and set the tip of his blade under its chin.

"You do not fear losing your head, fellow, is that it?"

"No, sir," it rasped, in that raw, irritating manner.

Rhalgorn raised a brow. "You don't? Then, you are even

more ignorant than I imagined, or you are lying, as I have suspected all along."

"No, sir," said the Metal-Man.

"No, sir, what?"

"No, sir, I am not lying."

"Hah!" Rhalgorn laughed ruefully. "You'd *say* that, wouldn't you!"

"Say what, sir?"

"Say that—say that you were—that you do not care whether I split your foolish head!"

"No, sir."

"No, sir, what!" Rhalgorn's red eyes narrowed. Long teeth curled 'round his muzzle. "Would you have me believe you do not *like* staying alive, then? That the thought of being suddenly *dead* does not alarm you?"

"No, sir. I cannot like staying alive," it said, "for I do not have the function of liking, nor am I alive. Being dead, therefore, does not alarm me, for I do not have the function of being alarmed, nor could I be alarmed about being dead if I did have such a function, because, as I said—"

If I had not stepped in at that moment, I am certain Rhalgorn would have cleaved the Metal-Man in quarters, then bounded off in search of the others.

Thus, I learned there was indeed a tenth level in Amazon Keep, and that there seemed no way to enter it. And while I did not learn how one communicates rationally with Metal-Men, I learned still another way that one does not.

I will say this for Stygianns—they are as stubborn as they are nosy. Once they are firmly set upon a matter, they do not give up without a fight. If one is determined that a stump should fly like a bird, then he will sit all day and watch it, certain that it will soon sprout wings.

In the days to come, Rhalgorn dogged Stumbaucius relentlessly, driving him near to madness, no doubt, for he had decided that he would bend these curious metal creatures to his will. He claimed this was a very serious scientific endeavor, but the truth of the matter is he simply would not admit there was a being of *any* sort on earth who could out-talk a seasoned Stygiann warrior.

Thirty

Nothing born of the Creator has a sharper ear—or quicker tongue—than the idle warrior. I did not mention our discovery of a tenth level, nor did Stumbaucius or Rhalgorn. My orders were specific on this, and they did not disobey me. Yet, within the hour the news had spread to every corner of the Keep. Even the lowliest soldier or sailor knew the lurid details of this latest "mystery of Man." There were no details to know, of course, but this did not stop Barthius or Sha'diir. There was a dungeon—nay, a pit, below Amazon Keep, black as the depths of Hell and full to the brim with unspeakable horrors. Several fellows had heard gruesome noises emanating from this place, and one had actually *seen* me on its brink, calling forth great monsters to my bidding.

This last was more than I could bear. Ignoring Corysia's very valid reasons why I should stay where I was, I stormed down to the big room where the company took its meals and demanded the fellow who'd seen this spectacle tell it to my face. It was a fool's errand, of course, for no such person existed outside Barthius' imagination.

"Listen to me," I told them, "and if you will listen to me no longer, listen to those among you who still have their wits about them! Give no ear to any who would use you to *their* ends, and not your own!"

Angry voices met my words, but these were clearly mixed with cheers for what I had to say. Fists flailed the air—a mug suddenly hit the wall beside me, shattered, and splattered me with wine. Some of the crewmen roared with pleasure at this, but not for long. A big Vikonen found the culprit and knocked him to the floor with the back of his hand. For a moment, I thought the rebellion might begin right then and there.

"Wait!" I shouted, bounding atop a table, "wait, and hear me out!" The room quieted, for there were still more loyal

folk than rebels among them. "I ask you to reason with me,"
I said. "I ask you to have a care that you do not throw away
what you have gained. We have a chance for a new beginning
here—a start on a life untarnished by the past. In time, the
world can be *our* world again—a world that—"

"What kind of world is this?" someone yelled. "It don't
look like *our* world, for sure!"

Voices filled the hall again, and this time it took somewhat
longer to quiet them. "I know you miss your homes," I said.
"I miss mine, as well. But the lands across the sea are *not*
our homes any longer! That world is a dead world. This one
belongs to us!"

They howled at this, but I would not let them stop me.
"You are thinking only of today and not tomorrow!" I told
them, shouting to make myself heard. "You are thinking of
this land as it is, not as it could be."

"Can it be the sands of Niciea!" yelled one.

"Can you turn this stinkin' place into the northlands!"
said another.

"No. I cannot. But I can bring much of the old world to
this one. I can bring the ways and the *people* that make a
place worth calling home." I stopped, and gave them the best
broad smile I could manage. "Would you find this world any
better if there were *females* in it? Answer me that!"

For the small part of a second the hall was deadly still.
Then, they realized what I'd said, and came to their feet as
one. Fear and anger turned to raucous cheers and hearty
laughter. They took me to their shoulders and hailed me once
again as their friend and leader. Only a handful of sullen
warriors and seamen stood their ground about Barthius and
Sha'diir, for my words had touched a hunger in their souls far
greater than any other.

Thus, I brought hope to the hearts of the crew, and peace
to Amazon Keep. It was an uneasy peace, and I was under
no illusion that it would last. We had slowed Barthius down
a bit, but I was certain he would not give up so easily. Indeed, no more than a day or so later he was using my own
words against me, telling the crew that all I said was a lie,
that I had no intention of sending the *Ahzir* across the sea
for females or anything else.

Signar was near bursting with anger; if he had had his

way, Barthius and his followers would have seen the end
of rope before the day was done.

"Damn, Aldair," he raged, "what is it you're waitin' for?
If there was ever a clearer case for mutiny, I'd like to see it!"

"The case is clear enough," I agreed, "and I have no qualms
about putting the fellow to his death. Not anymore. It is the
others I'm thinking about, Signar. We cannot take Barthius
down without condemning a great many others as well. There
are many among his followers who fought long and coura-
geously in our cause. I do not wish to see them die simply
because they have been taken in by foolish talk."

"Foolish talk, is it?" The Vikonen made no attempt to hide
his disgust. "That *foolish talk* is a sword at your throat,
Aldair. That devil means to have his way, and he'll not stop
now till our own blood's on the walls of Amazon Keep—you
can mark my words on that!"

Still, I would not give the command to send Barthius and
his followers to their deaths. Instead, to show that my words
were true, I hurried repairs on the *Ahzir al'Rhaz*, and set the
crew to work gathering the goods and provisions for a long
voyage across the Misty Sea. I was quite sincere about this
plan, though I am sure there were many among the crew who
believed I made it up on the spot to save my head. In truth,
it was the only rational thing to do if one stopped to think
about it. If we could not survive in the Old World, we would
have to make our way somewhere else—and where better than
Amazon Keep? Perhaps the climate was not all it could be,
but there were no empires to fear, and no wars to fight. We
were neither hungry nor thirsty here, and if the ancient charts
of Man were true, there was land a'plenty on the southern
continent.

Certainly, I have not accomplished all I've set out to do,
for a great part of the world is either dead or bound to the
chains of the past, cursed to relieve the terrible history of
Man. I have not yet broken that chain, and perhaps I never
will. But I have done something else—I have found a fair
way to go around it, a way to start again, to build a new
world unfettered by the old. And I am determined not to let
that chance slip away, merely because a few malcontents and
fools would bring me down.

The grumbling among the crew continued, and if I imagined it would lessen with the hope of something better on the horizon, I was sadly disappointed. More fights broke out between Barthius' followers and my own. Rumors spread like wildfire. The *Ahzir* would sail, all right, but common crewmen would not be aboard. *I* would be at the helm, with a crew of demons from my famous "pit," and the hold would be bursting to the seams with gold and gems and other great treasures supposedly found in Amazon Keep.

Inevitably, as good Signar had predicted, I was forced to take strong measures. Barthius and Sha'diir, grown bold by my inaction, coolly murdered two Niciean sailors who refused to join their camp. With a guard of loyal Vikonen warriors at my back, I marched into common quarters and took Barthius, Sha'diir, and seven of their followers. All were placed in irons, and I announced openly that they would be hanged for their crimes before the week was out, and that there was ample room on the gallows for any who cared to join them.

"You're makin' a mistake," warned Signar, "waitin' any time at all to string up those devils. Do it, and have it done!"

"Why?" I asked. "We've gotten the rotten apples out of the barrel."

"Maybe," put in Rhalgorn.

"You think there are more?" I turned to the Stygiann. "And if there are, why, we have the leaders and their most ardent followers. Isn't that enough? By damn, Rhalgorn—I won't kill every member of our band to be certain there's not another dissenter among them! Nine more deaths on my hands are all I can stomach, and then some!"

Signar shook his head savagely. "They're not on *your* hands, Aldair. They brought it on themselves!"

"They did, for sure," added the Stygiann.

"I have said all I care to say," I told them. "The matter is closed and that's the end of it."

"I hope to all the gods you're right," Signar muttered darkly, "but I'm certain as sin you ain't, Aldair."

To tell the truth, I was not nearly as sure of myself as I led the others to believe. I simply could not come 'round to more killing, even vermin like Barthius and Sha'diir, for I had had my fill of it. If this was a weakness on my part—then so be it. I had fought this weakness before, and brought us to

Amazon Keep. Wasn't that enough? Did I have to prove myself again?

Strange talk, perhaps, for one brought up in the warrior trade. But even a stone is not simply that and nothing more—it has both darkness and light within it, and veins of every color.

"Am I wrong?" I asked Corysia. "I have been a fool before, more than once, and it would not surprise me to find I've taken that cast again."

"Do you *think* you're a fool?" she said gently.

"I think I must be what I am, but I am not wholly certain I have the right to such a luxury. The decisions I make affect others besides myself."

"True. But I do not think any of us could accuse you of putting yourself before the common good, Aldair. You are surely not as fine and noble as you would wish to be—or that you *demand* you be—but you have not done badly for us."

"There are some who would disagree with you," I reminded her. "A few of these are out there howling for my skin. And there are others who are no longer alive to complain about my decisions."

She was silent a long moment. Then her hand reached out and found mine. "That is ever with you, is it not, my love? In the Creator's name, Aldair—make peace with yourself. Neither your companions nor your lover can do it for you!"

"I am more than tired," I told her. "I would see an end to this business soon, Corysia, but there seems no way to bring such an end about. . . ."

"There ever comes a time," Rhalgorn announced, "when those who have laughed at their betters find themselves laughing out of the other side of their snouts. This is an old saying among the Lords of the Lauvectii."

We had pushed the supper dishes aside to enjoy a cup of ale when the Stygiann suddenly made this pronouncement. "What on earth are you talking about," laughed Corysia, "Stygianns do not *have* snouts, and that is certainly not one of their sayings!"

"Thank the gods we do not, Lady—begging your pardon —but we have neighbors of a sort who *do*," he looked pointedly at me, "and they are a proud and haughty lot."

"Rhalgorn," I said, pushing back my chair, "you've got something to say, for sure, but there's not a person here has the slightest idea what it is."

"Of course you don't," he said, sniffling the air with great disdain, "for you have closed your tiny pink ear to Rhalgorn, who is only a savage from the eastern woods and not fit for proper thinking."

"It's no use," Thareesh said wearily, "he won't get to it till he's ready."

Signar scratched his furry belly and yawned. "I, for one, don't figure on waitin' 'round to see. If you'll excuse me, Lady—"

Rhalgorn laughed, that peculiar coughing sound that passes for laughter among the Stygianns. "Wait, fat-fur—for you I'll tell it all, and quickly!"

"Don't do me no favors," growled Signar.

"Ah, but I will. Not for you, Aldair—for you ever scoff at Rhalgorn's efforts, an act which pains me greatly, by the way."

"I can imagine. And what efforts are you talking about—if any?"

Rhalgorn grinned through his long muzzle, looking very much as if he'd just finished a fine hare. "If any, is it? You will not say that when you learn I have solved the secret of the tenth level of Amazon Keep!"

I nearly knocked my mug to the floor. "What are you talking about?"

"I mean," he said smugly, "I know how to get *in*."

"You know how. But you haven't actually done it."

"It's the same thing."

"Indeed it is not."

"If you *know* something, it is as good as done, Aldair."

"For Stygianns, maybe. But not for other folk, who like to *see* things rather than hear how they might be accomplished."

"Why don't you both quit talking aboout it?" hissed Thareesh. He pulled himself erect and switched his thin Nicean tail. "There is a very simple way to end this conversation."

"They could both stop jawing, for one thing," suggested the Vikonen.

"Better still," said Thareesh, "let us all go see this marvel now. Rhalgorn?"

Rhalgorn beamed and looked at me. "Go ahead," I told him. "You got yourself into this."

"And gladly so," said the Stygiann. "Fat-fur, I will need your help in this. If nothing else, you have strong broad shoulders."

Signar gave him a blood-red look. "To do what?"

"Why, to carry good Wall-drop, of course."

I stopped, halfway in my jacket. "Rhalgorn, what does *Wall*-drop have to do with this?"

Rhalgorn grinned. "Everything, Aldair, as you will see in good time. . . ."

Thirty-one

———— ⋈ ⋖═⋗ ⋈ ————

"Rhalgorn, you are making a great fool of yourself. I intend to remind you of this day many times in the years to come."

Rhalgorn showed me a crooked grin. "We will see who does the reminding, Aldair."

"Where do you want this lovely feller?" asked Signar-Haldring. A broad smile crossed his features, for he was enjoying this business immensely. In his big arms he held the limp form of the Metal-Man that Stumbaucius had christened Wall-drop.

"Just there will be fine," Rhalgorn said coolly. "We will get to him shortly."

Signar stood back and studied the thing on the floor. "You figure ol' Wall-drop'll sing us a tune, Aldair, or maybe do a little dance? Can't say which would please me most."

"He will do a great deal more than that," said Rhalgorn. "He will open that door is what he'll do."

"You have absolutely no reason to believe that," I said.

"I have every reason in the world, Aldair. It is simply a matter of logic."

"*Stygiann* logic?"

"Of course."

"Well, that explains a great deal."

"It does, though you say it in jest. I have studied the tin creatures thoroughly, and I have learned a great deal about them."

"Such as?" asked Thareesh.

"Such as the fact that they *do* things."

"Of course they do things," I said. "We already know that."

He shook his head. "I mean, they do *certain* things. Stumbaucius told you this but you failed to listen. Some carry things. Some know where things are kept. Another does noth-

170

ing but make sure the little Man-suns are working. Wall-drop,
here, opens doors."

"What?" I stared at him. "You've never seen Wall-drop
open a door and you never will. He's *broken*, Rhalgorn. He
doesn't do anything."

"He is not broken," Rhalgorn said flatly.

"He looks broken to me."

"As you yourself said, he is not *doing* anything. That is not
the same as being broken. The others keep working—or pre-
tend to—because no one told them to stop. Wall-drop stopped
because he had nothing to do."

"Rhalgorn—!"

"The other Metal-Men open doors," he explained, "but I
am not talking about that kind of opening. I have watched
them. They will open doors that are unlocked, but they will
not bother with the others. I have asked them to, but they will
not. Because they don't know how. Wall-drop does."

I waited, but he was evidently finished for the moment.
"That's it? This is what you brought us down here for? To
listen to some—patchwork Stygiann logic!"

"I brought you down here to open a door," sniffled Rhalgorn.

"Fine," I said. "Go ahead, seer of the Lauvectii. We are
waiting."

I think Rhalgorn would have gladly stopped this nonsense
then and there. Stygianns are the most arrogant braggarts ever
conceived by the Creator, but they would rather die in battle
than appear foolish.

Trying hard to look solemn, Signar dutifully followed Rhalgorn's instructions. He carried Wall-drop to the door and held
him straight. Wall-drop's head sagged. His limp metal feet
dragged on the floor. Rhalgorn stood back and studied the
situation a moment. Finally, he said, "Now, Wall-drop—open
this door for us."

Wall-drop continued to sag.

"Perhaps he doesn't know his name," Thareesh suggested.

"That's right," I added. Stumbaucius gave him this name.
He probably had another before. Try some different names,
Rhalgorn."

"Aldair," Corysia said firmly, "just leave him alone."

"I am only trying to help, Corysia."

"That is not what you are trying to do."

"His name has no bearing whatever," Rhalgorn said darkly. "You—whatever you are called. Open this door at *once!*"

Signar could contain himself no longer. He gave a loud burst of laughter that shook the room.

Rhalgorn ignored him. "Move the creature up a little closer, please. He is too far away."

Signar bristled. I ain't plannin' on holding this thing all day Rhalgorn.

"Only a moment more. . . ." He frowned thoughtfully, then a big grin split his muzzle. "Ah, of course. How foolish of me. Creatures do not simply stand before doors. They must touch them before they open!"

"There is no knob on the door to touch," I pointed out, "you may have noticed this before."

Rhalgorn wasn't listening. He grasped the thing's left hand and pressed it against the metal.

Wall-drop continued to sag.

"If you will stop this nonsense now," I said, "we will all promise never to mention it again."

"*I* won't" said Signar.

"Must be he's right-handed," said Thareesh.

"Exactly what I was thinking," said Rhalgorn. With that, he raised the limp right hand of the Metal-Man and held it against the door.

Wall-drop went suddenly rigid. Tiny blue hairs of lightning crackled across his body. Rhalgorn and Signar howled. Their fur stood on end. A great invisible club picked them off their feet and tossed them to the floor.

Wall-drop swayed dangerously, then righted himself. His hand moved smoothly over the door, paused, then stopped. He took a shaky step to the left, and tried again. For a long moment, nothing happened. Then, before our unbelieving eyes, the door slid aside with a whisper.

"Creator's Eyes," said Signar. "I ain't seein' this, for certain."

Rhalgorn picked himself up. "What—what did you expect, fat-fur?" He was trying very hard to hide his own astonishment. "I said it would open and it—opened. I—"

"Shut up, the both of you!" I said, for I was already past them, staring at the sight before me. . . .

How can I say what I saw there, and give meaning to the

words? It was a vast, open chamber, bound on every side by pale, milky walls that seemed to flee from one another then arc to the heights in quick, sweeping curves that wondrously met again. There were clusters of golden spheres about the surface of the room, each the same as the other, and each more than three meters high. These spheres were grouped in circles of seven, and there were seven circles in all. Not all the circles were complete, for out of forty-nine spheres that would have made the pattern whole, fully a quarter were no longer there. The room, the walls, the golden spheres—all were lit by the chill-cold glare of Man-suns, through I couldn't guess where even one of these devices might be placed.

Thus, I have described as best I can the room behind the door on the tenth level of Amazon Keep. In truth, I have said next to nothing, for there were things within that place we could neither touch nor see nor scarce imagine.

"I'm frightened, Aldair. I'm frightened out of my wits and I can't say why." Corysia pressed herself against me, gripping my hand in hers.

"I feel it," I said, "it is a thing that is here, and yet is not." I caught myself near whispering the words, for it was somehow a fearsome thing to speak in that place.

Glancing about, I found Rhalgorn, Signar and Thareesh. They were there beside me, but I could not be sure whether they were real and solid beings or mere shades of themselves. It seemed as if the tiny shards of every moment, day and hour that ever were flew thick about us, like the motes of a dusty summer.

"Time is out of tune here," Thareesh said later, and I can put it no bettter than that.

Something made me turn at that moment; I caught a quick glimpse of motion from the corner of my eye. Jerking full around I saw the Stygiann, and knew what he was about. "Rhalgorn!" I yelled, shattering the deadly silence. "Rhalgorn, no! *Get away from that!*"

He stopped, just short of a golden sphere. There was a curious, bewildered look across his features, as if I'd spoken in some foreign tongue. I moved to his side as quickly as I could, cursing the peculiar nature of the place that turned my boots to lead.

"Don't touch it," I warned. "Don't even get near it, Rhalgorn. Look—" I pointed to the sphere before us. "By all the gods, it's not even as it seems!"

Indeed, this close the thing was not the solid object it appeared to be, but an illusive circle of silver, pearl and gold spun thin as gauze—a mere shadow of something else we could not fathom. As I watched, it wavered, changed. It was a most pleasurable thing, to gaze at this marvel and know the slow, windless currents of the immeasurable years. . . .

"*Aldair!*" I blinked, coming suddenly back from nowhere.

"We've—got to get out of here," said Rhalgorn, "—now!"

"Yes. . . ." I tried to put the words together. "Get—out of here. . . ."

Suddenly I was off the ground, slung roughly over his shoulder. Corysia? Where was she? Signar, Thareesh. . . .?

It was over.

I was out of that terrible chamber, my companions by my side. We neither spoke nor glanced at one another until we reached the top of those narrow stairs and left the tenth level of Amazon Keep far behind. . . .

Thirty-two

Soldiers will sit apart from one another after tragedy has touched them. Stunned and silent, they do not speak to their companions or look them in the eyes—for that would make the thing that has happened to them real again.

We had left level ten behind, but we could not as easily shake the feel of it. It was much like a dream that won't give up its hold, but clings long after sleep is done.

"Whatever all that was done there," said Signar, "I don't much care 'bout seein' it twice." He downed a mug of wine and made a face. "*Once* was more'n I like to remember."

"Yes," said Corysia, "more than enough for us all." I held her close against me, but this did not stop her trembling.

Thareesh shook his head and frowned thoughtfully. "They were—much like the golden craft by the river—weren't they? Did you notice that? Like it—but not the same."

"No," I said, "not the same at all. The craft by the river is real. I've touched it, and I know it's there. I am not at all certain what is there and not there down below."

"When I think back upon it," said the Nicician, "I cannot easily remember even *being* there. That is most peculiar, Aldair. It is like nothing I have ever experienced."

I caught his gaze and held it. "It is, Thareesh. Very much like something you've experienced. Have you forgotten the Eye of Man—the terrible device that brought madness to Rhemia's capital? It is not the same as that, or the machines we're certain chart the course of history. But it is not all that *different*, either."

One look at my companions told me they knew exactly what I was saying. "The devices of Man seem much alike in one respect—they do little to improve the reason, which is no doubt what he had in mind. Clearly, we have not discovered a

175

better, more rational breed of that race—only more of the same!"

"I am not at all sure that's true," said Corysia.

"And I'm not at all sure it's not!" I said, though my anger was not meant for her. "Rhalgorn—that door must not remain open. We ran from that place like frightened hares. Now, it is time we got our wits about us. Wall-drop opened the damn thing—now he can close it again."

Rhalgorn nodded, and pulled himself erect. "Wait," I told him. "When the place is closed, make certain the Metal-Man is not available to practice his art. I do not want that chamber opened. By anyone. And Signar—put guards at the tenth level. Even if the place is shut tight, I want no one near it."

"Who d'you suggest?" asked Signar. "I *think* I know who we can trust, but they're all of 'em acting peculiar these days."

I shook my head and sat down. "Creator's Breath, it makes no difference one way or the other, does it? They'll all know soon enough. They always do. Barthius will simply have a few *more* demons to howl at!"

With Signar and Rhalgorn gone, I sat in silence, studying the dregs of my wine. Like myself, neither Corysia nor Thareesh had much to say. What *was* there to say, that had much meaning?

"Forgive my anger," I told her, "it was not for you."

"I'm not concerned with your anger," she said. "I still question your logic, Aldair. I will probably dream about that place the rest of my days, but my fears or yours do *not* prove the Men of Amazon Keep were like the rest—only that we didn't understand what we saw down there."

"Corysia—" I tried hard to hold my patience. "What do you think that *was* down there?"

"I have no idea. And neither do you. But I cannot forget what you were told by the Por'ai. We were *supposed* to find Amazon Keep—remember? If the sea-folk are what you say they are, would they send us into danger?"

"The Por'ai don't know everything, Corysia. And you'll recall we've been a great many places we were supposed to be, if you can believe there's some guidance to this venture. Most of them were quite unpleasant, and deadly to boot."

"I know," she sighed, "still—"

"I simply can't forget how I felt down there. Can you? I didn't know where I was or what I was seeing. More than that,

I was not even certain of the *when* of it all, for time has a season of its own down there. To me, that was the most frightening thing of all. What in the Creator's name have we unearthed here? If time itself bows to the rule of Man, who can stand against him?"

No one moved to answer that question, which did not surprise me. Moreover, at that moment Rhalgorn appeared again, back from his mission. Without a word, he sat himself down and emptied the largest mug of wine he could find.

"I regret to tell you Wall-drop is not as good at closing doors as he is at opening them," he said wearily. "Or if he is, he is clearly not in the mood for it. I suppose I will get the blame for all this—that is ever the lot of those who point the way for others. . . ."

Thirty-three

As expected, rumors concerning the tenth level were not long in coming. This time it was easier for the rebels to frighten the crew, for they had something genuinely fearsome to work with.

Once again, I cursed my weakness in dealing with these mutineers. Even in irons awaiting death, Barthius was dangerous. We had rounded up his most ardent followers, but we'd clearly not taken them all. The remaining malcontents were more cautious in their actions, making them all that harder to find.

I did what I could. I talked to those who would listen. I set the *Ahzir's* sailing date forward, hoping this would give them something to look forward to. I am not certain I made any converts. Those who wanted to listen to reason listened. The others, I am sure, ignored me. This new tenth level business did little to help matters. I had forbidden passage beyond the stairs *leading* to that place. But they knew what was there. Those who got a quick look at the golden sphere had much to tell their mates.

Thus, if there had ever been a chance to quell rebellion, I believe that chance had passed. Master Aldair had lied, had he not? He said there was nothing to fear in Amazon Keep—what *else* did this friend of demons have in store?

One morning, there was a crude drawing of myself on the outer wall. I had horns for ears and a wart on my snout. My tail was longer, with a wicked barb at its tip.

"At least, they do not defame Stygianns," noted Rhalgorn. "I suppose they don't dare to."

"They don't *have* to," I said. "Stygianns look close enough to demons as it is."

He thought about that. "Do you truly think so? It is something I had never considered." Clearly, he was quite taken with the idea, and bored me with it the rest of the day.

It happened, as we knew it would, but not at all in the way we expected. Signar was certain they'd try for Barthius that day, as he was set for execution on the morrow. I agreed. We were wrong.

Showing themselves for the cowards they were, they made no effort to save their leader. Instead, they decided if they were still around after Barthius died, there were those among the crew who'd gladly have their heads—if I didn't claim them first. Thus, they decided to turn double-traitor and make a profit in the bargain. All this I deduced through the great clarity of hindsight, when I learned the rebels had boarded the *Ahzir al'Rhaz* and were near to taking it from us.

"If one of those devils mars a plank on that ship I'll have their ears for breakfast!" raged Signar. He bounded down the trail ahead of me like a great oak uprooted. The fur stood straight up on his back and his war-axe whistled above his head. Friend or foe, it seemed prudent to be at his heels for the moment.

We could hear the howl of battle, the ring-song of metal on metal. The dull brown of the river came to view, and there stood Rhalgorn, leaning comfortably on his sword.

"You are late, fat-fur," he grinned. "It is near finished, and you'll have no need to dent that cleaver of yours."

"Finished?" Signar's jaw fell in disappointment. He glanced at the *Ahzir*, which was moored quite close to shore now. In truth, there was little action aboard, though I heard a great deal of cursing and shouting going on.

"Well, by damn, we're goin' out there anyway," growled the Vikonen. "All that fightin' they likely broke something. Folks got no respect for a fine ship, and that's for certain!"

Thareesh was the only one of us who'd been near enough to take part in the encounter, for it was indeed a short-lived battle. There was a bit of blood on the decks, and a few arrows stuck about. Otherwise, it seemed a bright and steamy afternoon on the River Amazon.

"We were lucky there were a few loyal warriors lazing about the shore," said Thareesh, "or we'd have lost the ship for sure."

Signar discovered there had been perhaps fourteen rebels

involved—one being a guard on the ship. Three were killed and one wounded.

The others, appalled to find resistance pulling swiftly out from shore, fled the *Ahzir* in a longboat and took shelter on the farther bank.

"You goin' after 'em?" asked Signar. "They can't have gotten far."

"No," I told him, "they are so eager to fight something, let them have a try at the wilderness out there. I do not think they'll relish what they find."

When Barthius heard of his followers' betrayal, he howled and cursed and jerked at his irons until blood flowed from his wrists. The guards restrained him, tightening his chains so he could not thrash about. "You must not injure yourself," they told him, "for the rope awaits you in the morning." These were Vikonen from the cold lands beyond Vhiborg, and it is their belief that it is extremely bad luck to hang a creature who is not in good health.

Sha'diir and the others said nothing. There was neither hope nor rebellion in them now. Their eyes already mirrored the flat, gray luster of death.

"Damned if I've ever enjoyed a swallow of ale more'n that one!" shouted Signar-Haldring.

"If that's a swallow, then I'm a hare in a hollow," said Rhalgorn, spilling most of his cup on his pelt. Signar laughed and near fell out of his chair. It was a sound measure of how much they'd had to drink, if these two found each other amusing.

"A toast!" cried Thareesh, "to Aldair!"

"To Aldair!" echoed the others.

I laughed, and raised my drink to theirs. . . .

"You do not have to leave," she told me. "I can find my way alone."

"They will never miss us," I grinned. "From the sound of things they'll go on into the dawn, or till the kegs go dry."

She stopped then, and her hand was suddenly cold in mine.

"Corysia? What's wrong?" From the far end of the hall I heard Signar's deep-throated laughter.

"Nothing, I—" She turned away, dropping my hand. "As you said, until the dawn. And then—I am not a warrior,

Aldair. I cannot enjoy good company and think about the morrow at the same time."

"Barthius and the others."

She nodded. "I know it has to be."

"It does, Corysia."

"But I do not have to enjoy it."

"None of us will enjoy it. But if it didn't end this way, it would end in another. They would see us all on the gallows— or worse."

"I know."

I laughed a little and touched her cheek. "You are talking like Aldair himself, now."

"And why not?" She raised a brow and dared me to fault it. "I spend a great deal of time with that Aldair. It is no wonder I'm growing like him."

"The gods forbid!" I said.

"Not *entirely* like him."

"Let us hope not. Let us hope you retain certain features of your own. I would be most displeased if you did not."

"And so would I," she said.

"It is a fair arrangement, and I have no desire to change it."

"Only fair?"

"Well, perhaps excellent would be more appropriate."

"Yes, I think so. At least excellent. . . ."

We stood there a long moment, holding one another and saying nothing, savoring a silence that needed no words. I left her, assuring her I would only be a minute, and she said she'd very likely be there if it was no longer than that.

From the high window at the end of the corridor I smelled the rich, wet odor of the night, and saw the bright, cold points of a million stars. I know the southern sky, but I will never get used to its unfamiliar patterns. There is no Lame Warrior to point the way; the misty band of the Slave's Chain is lost beyond the horizon.

Would I see those sights again, I wondered—the skies I knew so well, and the lands beneath them? It is best to put such thoughts aside, for the lands I know are not as I remember them, and I do not care to picture them as they are.

From the far end of the hall came a loud burst of laughter, then another. I grinned to myself. They would rue this night

tomorrow, but the day to come is not the proper concern for
warriors with a keg of wine.

The laughter came again, louder this time. Damn me, I
thought, were they taking the Keep apart? If Signar—

Again, but this time another sound laced through the first—
one that set my hair on end. That was no laughter, it was the
howl of battle—and the other voice was Corysia's!

"Corysia!" I was down the hall, boots ringing on hollow
stone. Again I heard her, and this time with the unmistakable
sound of one blade set against another.

Rounding a corner, I came up hard against them. Two
Vikonen and a Niciean soldier. For the smallest part of a
second they stopped, surprised to find me. Then all three were
on me, weapons at the ready. A Vikonen axe whistled past my
head, I ducked beneath it, feinted to the left, and put the
Niciean between myself and the others. The fellow's blade
slashed down. I met it, turned it back, whipped my sword
'round in a short, curving sweep. He gasped, staggered back,
holding an empty sleeve. It is no shame to run from two
Vikonen warriors.

"Aldair, here!" Rhalgorn bounded into the hall from the
stairs above. Behind him, a loyal band of warriors spilled into
the passageway. At his quick direction, half went after the
rebel Vikonen, the rest spread out around us.

"Corysia," I said, "Rhalgorn, she's—"

"She is gone, Aldair," he said darkly. "I looked. Only minutes ago."

"Gone!"

"They have her, but we'll get her back. I swear it, Aldair."
He pulled me along beside him. I stopped, jerked away. "Rhalgorn—we will get her *now!*"

"We will get her when we can!" he said sharply. "Look, my
friend, we have been tricked, taken in. That business with the
ship was no more than a ruse to put us at our ease. And it
worked very nicely indeed!"

I stared. "The rebels who went after *Ahzir?*"

"No, I don't think they are even in this fray. There are
others, more than we imagined. The devils didn't show themselves till now—I'd guess they even *helped* us rout the others!"

A chill touched my spine. "Then they've freed Barthius.
If he's got Corysia, Rhalgorn—"

"If he's got her, we'll get her back."

One of our own shouted a warning. From a hall to our left came a horde of rebel warriors. We raised our battle cries and were on them long before they got their wits about them. My blade passed cleanly through a Niciean and I was gone before he fell. A big Vikonen loomed high over my head. With a howl that shook my skull, he cleaved the fellow behind me near in two, then aimed a heavy boot in my direction. I moved, but not fast enough. It caught my shoulder square and sent me sprawling. He was on me like a darkening cloud; I gripped my blade in both hands and blindly struck upward. The warrior roared, clutching his stomach. A great fount of blood spattered my chest—he reeled, drunkenly, snapping the blade at the hilt against the wall. I heard my name and a crewman I never saw thrust a new weapon in my hand.

Suddenly, we were through them. Not many rose to flee, and some of our own lay still among them.

Signar and Thareesh met us at the stairs, a small force of their own behind them. The Vikonen was covered with blood, but not a drop was his own. "They're all down that way," he shouted, "the main lot of 'em!"

"Did you see Corysia?"

He shook his great head. "I didn't, Aldair, but Barthius is loose down below, I know that, for sure."

"Then Corysia's there too."

"That's likely—he's got Sha'diir and the worst of 'em right with him. We hit the tail end of his crew back there a ways."

"Not Sha'diir," hissed Thareesh. His black-agate eyes were cold with anger. "I have finished that one myself!"

His words trailed off behind me for I was down the stairs and gone. I could see nothing before me but Barthius and Corysia. I was blind to all else. A cold blade of ice found my stomach and stayed there.

"Damn it all," said Signar, grabbing my shoulder hard in his big fist, "you ain't going to get there any quicker than the rest of us!"

I shook him off. "Rhalgorn—check the floor. Send warriors down that hallway."

In minutes they were back. There was not a rebel in sight. The ice-blade grew sharper inside. "Creator's Eyes, they've gone down again—to the tenth level!"

They were there, and waiting for us. A volley of arrows

whispered up the stairs to meet us. A great Vikonen, one of Sergrid Bad-Beard's exiles, took them on his shield and laughed. The rebels had formed a blade-wall to meet us, but we were on them like a river—cutting, slicing, hacking a death-line through their numbers. Signar carved his own path into the pack, leaving darkness in his wake. . . . Thareesh was an angry blur of green making bright new throats wherever he touched. . . . And Rhalgorn, that gray and silent wraith who brings death as quick as a shadow—he they feared most of all. Even the great Vikonen shrank from his presence, for a Stygi-ann warrior is the soul-killer, the night-bringer, the grave-maker of the world. . . .

I spotted Barthius near the far edge of the fighting. A war-rior barred my way, and when I looked again he was gone. A blade hit flat against my helm, near knocking me senseless. I turned, drove the fellow back, and I was through them all.

Barthius saw me, grinned, stood his ground a moment, then ran for the shadows. I started for him, stopped—and went suddenly cold all over. When he turned again she was there, hard against him. One arm grasped her waist, the other held a small, thin blade to her throat.

"*Don't*, Master Aldair," he said calmly, "you know I will do it, and gladly!"

"Put her aside, Barthius."

He laughed. "Not likely, *Master* Aldair."

"It is not her fight. It is ours. Yours and mine." I moved a step closer. His eyes went dark with anger and he brought the blade up tight against her skin.

"It's her death if you come farther," he shouted, "I'll kill her certain!"

I didn't stop. I took one step—another. He stared as if I'd lost my senses.

"Don't!"

"I will. I'm coming for you, Barthius."

"I'll—kill her. I'll do it sure!"

"No, you will not. For when you do you kill yourself. You are a coward, and you do not wish to die. Not the way *I* will make you die." I prayed he couldn't see the fear that held me, for it had to be this way. If I gave ground, did as he asked—she was dead.

He searched about, frantically. There was no help coming. His friends had troubles of their own. He moved back, another step, glanced over his shoulder and tightened his grip on Corysia. The ice-blade touched my spine and I suddenly *knew* what he was doing—he had no intention of making for the stairs or anywhere else. He was angling the other way, and there was nothing in his path but the door to the chamber itself.

I stopped. "Don't, Barthius!"

He looked up, then behind him. A half-smile creased his face.

"Don't want me to see what you got in there, Master Aldair?"

"You cannot know what's in there. You don't want to."

"But I do!"

"Barthius, *listen* to me!"

He moved away quickly, pulling her through the open portal. Corysia's eyes went wide and I knew I could wait no longer. Whatever happened, I could *not* let him take her in there! I ran, not thinking what he might do. I could already sense the terrible presence in that place.

He looked up, saw me. Knew only that I was coming for him. Bewilderment touched his features. Now, he could feel what was in there. Behind him loomed a golden sphere, aglow like the breath of a god.

"Barthius!"

He was too far away and I knew I could never get there. All I could do was watch as he stumbled blindly into the thing, taking Corysia with him.

Time shattered in a billion pieces, and they were gone.

A quick wink, a color that was no color at all. Where the golden sphere had been, there was nothing.

"Corysia!"

I called her name, but she did not answer.

"Corysia!"

I cried her name, but she could not hear.

"Corysia!"

I screamed a thousand screams, but she would not come. And if she would not, then I would go where she had gone.

"Aldair—by all the gods. . . !" Rhalgorn held me in fingers of iron. I shook him off, breathed gold and silver dust, and fell into tomorrow. . . .

Epilogue

"I suppose I will get the blame for all this," said Rhalgorn.

"I don't see how that will help a great deal," I told him. "However, if it makes you happy you may take the blame for whatever you wish. I'm really not interested, one way or the other."

"I don't *think* it was all my fault," he said after a while.

"Fine."

"I opened the door, with Wall-drop's help—but I did not ask people to walk into golden things. That was more or less *your* idea—"

"All right."

"—Not mine."

"All *right*, Rhalgorn . . ."

If time moved at all, it slipped so quietly by I never saw it pass. . . .

"Aldair, I wish to know exactly where we are. Stygianns have a fine sense of direction, but I must admit I am somewhat confused at the moment."

"As I have said before, we are precisely nowhere, Rhalgorn. That's as close as I can come."

"That does not make a great deal of sense," he said. "Everyone is somewhere."

"*That* does not make sense either," I told him, pointing past his shoulder. "Nevertheless, there it is."

For perhaps the ten-thousandth time since somewhen, I took in the scene outside the silk-silver walls of our golden sphere. It was the same as ever—an unfathomable number of bright-cold stars against a great, immeasurable darkness. Occasionally, we seemed to move against that darkness, but what we were moving to, or away from, I couldn't say. I watched, though, because there was nothing else to see.

"We will find her. . . ."

"What?"

"I said, we will find her. Corysia. I was talking to myself."

"Yes," he said, "we will, Aldair. . . ."

If seconds turned to centuries, they left so whisper-soft I scarcely heard them. . . .

"At least, we know where Man has gone—or how he got there, anyway. Though I'm not at all sure that's very helpful now."

Rhalgorn raised a brow. "You think so? He went somewhere in *this*?"

"It stands to reason that's what the spheres are for. Doesn't it?"

"It is not a very seemly way to travel," said Rhalgorn. "The best thing to go somewhere in is a thing one can steer. I see nothing of that nature here."

"Perhaps it doesn't need steering."

Rhalgorn made a face. "Aldair—*this* one does. . . ."

Corysia, Corysia . . . are you out here somewhere, drifting along some other crest of the Darker Sea?

I had created a most convenient fiction about that. Corysia had a sphere of her own—Barthius, through some happy error, was no longer with her.

"I wish I was back in the forests of the Lauvectii, Aldair."

"Sometimes, I wish you were too, Rhalgorn."

"There are probably fat hares about, now. And a good soft snow. Just right for tracking."

"Probably."

"I like the ones with the short pointy ears best of all. Don't you?"

"As you know, I don't much care for hares of any kind, Rhalgorn."

There is a song the ages sing, but if I stop too long to listen, it goes away. . . .

"We will find her, Aldair."

"I know."

"Perhaps, we will also find ourselves. I am convinced Man rode these things from one place to another. If he left the Earth behind, he surely had somewhere else to go. One does not just get in a something and go flit about the stars."

"I shouldn't think so."

"I am tired of sitting up here, Aldair. There is very little to do. We will find a place to take this thing. And we will find Corysia, as well."

"You are right. Those are two things we should do, Rhalgorn."

I think a moment passed . . . I caught just the tail of it from the corner of my eye. . . .

DRAY PRESCOT

The great novels of Kregen, world of Antares

Fully illustrated

If you wish to order these titles,

please use the coupon on

the last page of this book.

Recommended for Star Warriors!

The Novels of Gordon R. Dickson

☐ **DORSAI!** (#UE1342—$1.75)
☐ **SOLDIER, ASK NOT** (#UE1339—$1.75)
☐ **NECROMANCER** (#UE1481—$1.75)
☐ **HOUR OF THE HORDE** (#UE1514—$1.75)
☐ **THE STAR ROAD** (#UJ1526—$1.95)

The Commodore Grimes Novels of A. Bertram Chandler

☐ **THE WAY BACK** (#UW1352—$1.50)
☐ **TO KEEP THE SHIP** (#UE1385—$1.75)
☐ **THE FAR TRAVELER** (#UW1444—$1.50)
☐ **THE BROKEN CYCLE** (#UE1496—$1.75)

The Dumarest of Terra Novels of E. C. Tubb

☐ **INCIDENT ON ATH** (#UW1389—$1.50)
☐ **THE QUILLIAN SECTOR** (#UW1426—$1.50)
☐ **WEB OF SAND** (#UE1479—$1.75)
☐ **IDUNA'S UNIVERSE** (#UE1500—$1.75)

The Daedalus Novels of Brian M. Stableford

☐ **THE FLORIANS** (#UY1255—$1.25)
☐ **CRITICAL THRESHOLD** (#UY1282—$1.25)
☐ **WILDEBLOOD'S EMPIRE** (#UW1331—$1.50)
☐ **THE CITY OF THE SUN** (#UW1377—$1.50)
☐ **BALANCE OF POWER** (#UE1437—$1.75)
☐ **THE PARADOX OF THE SETS** (#UE1495—$1.75)

If you wish to order these titles,

please use the coupon in

the back of this book.

Presenting MICHAEL MOORCOCK
in DAW editions

The Elric Novels

☐ **ELRIC OF MELNIBONE**   (#UW1356—$1.50)
☐ **THE SAILOR ON THE SEAS OF FATE**   (#UW1434—$1.50)
☐ **THE WEIRD OF THE WHITE WOLF**   (#UW1390—$1.50)
☐ **THE VANISHING TOWER**   (#UW1406—$1.50)
☐ **THE BANE OF THE BLACK SWORD**   (#UW1421—$1.50)
☐ **STORMBRINGER**   (#UW1335—$1.50)

The Runestaff Novels

☐ **THE JEWEL IN THE SKULL**   (#UW1419—$1.50)
☐ **THE MAD GOD'S AMULET**   (#UW1391—$1.50)
☐ **THE SWORD OF THE DAWN**   (#UW1392—$1.50)
☐ **THE RUNESTAFF**   (#UW1422—$1.50)

The Oswald Bastable Novels

☐ **THE WARLORD OF THE AIR**   (#UW1380—$1.50)
☐ **THE LAND LEVIATHAN**   (#UW1448—$1.50)

The Michael Kane Novels

☐ **CITY OF THE BEAST**   (#UW1436—$1.50)
☐ **LORD OF THE SPIDERS**   (#UW1443—$1.50)
☐ **MASTERS OF THE PIT**   (#UW1450—$1.50)

Other Titles

☐ **LEGENDS FROM THE END OF TIME**   (#UY1281—$1.25)
☐ **A MESSIAH AT THE END OF TIME**   (#UW1358—$1.50)
☐ **DYING FOR TOMORROW**   (#UW1366—$1.50)
☐ **THE RITUALS OF INFINITY**   (#UW1404—$1.50)

If you wish to order these titles,

please see the coupon in

the back of this book.